"Shawgo's writing ca
A compelling story. I
—*Michael Cacciatore, MD, OB/GYN*

"Shawgo captures the true essence of what nursing is all about. Her first attempt at novel writing is an inspiration to the writer in all of us."
—*Patricia Hensley, BSN, RNC*

"Wonderfully written heroic saga of a woman's determination, strength, and resourcefulness in giving unselfishly on the battlefield while putting herself in danger."
—*Rosemarie Masetta, BSN, RN*

"I found the book engaging and difficult to put down. I felt like I was actually there."
—*Melanie Reis, CNM, ARNP*

"Janet's story line was captivating and beautifully illustrated the wonderful profession of nursing, which has no boundaries. After reading this book, anyone thinking of joining the nursing profession will have a solid conviction to pursue that career path."
—*Christopher Walker, MD, FACOG, FICS, Fellow of American College of Obstetrics and Gynecology, Fellow of International College of Surgeons*

"Look for Me is well-researched, skillfully written, and is an easy, entertaining read which stirs the emotions."
—*Kay Hornsby, retired teacher, Masters in Education*

A masterful and accurate depiction of the efforts and methods used by early midwives in the care of their patients.
—*Cindy Stokes RN, MSN, CNS, CNM*

A deep display of the enduring strength and compassion, which inspires care givers. I recommend this book, it is a true lesson and embracing story.
Caren J. Bock, BSN-RN, CPN Author of **Wings:…A Story of Transformation**

LOOK
FOR
ME

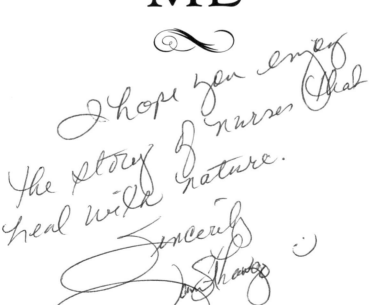

I hope you enjoy the story of nurses that heal with nature.

Sincerely,

LOOK
FOR
ME

JANET K. SHAWGO

Two Harbors Press
212 3rd Avenue North, Suite 290
Minneapolis, MN 55401
612.455.2293
www.TwoHarborsPress.com

ISBN-13: 978-1-937293-26-0
LCCN: 2011935618

Distributed by Itasca Books

Cover Design and Typeset by James Arneson

Printed in the United States of America

This book is dedicated
to my twin sister, Joan,
who sat patiently by my side
and reminded me that I cannot spell.
I love you, Sis.

Preface

I have often thought about individuals who write and what inspires them. There are personal causes, history, life experiences, the future, or their imagination—many subjects to choose from. My inspiration began in high school with a teacher who showed her students they could be whatever they chose. The creative writing class was filled with students who produced laughter and tears, and who challenged thought through the written word. I should have listened back then and walked down that road, but I chose another path.

The subject of a book should be one you are familiar with or know well. I began my research to see how far back I could find female healers, nurses. There are Biblical, Egyptian, and more, possibly into prehistoric times. Is this because women are nurturers? Is there some gene in our makeup that forces us to care for others? Is it a choice that we step out and go where others will not, into battle or the unknown?

The decision to write about travel nurses comes from over sixteen years as a traveler. I have met many wonderful travel nurses, staff nurses, midwives, and physicians who touched my heart and soul. I am proud to call them friends.

These women and men are characters and have left a mark on my life forever. When I became a travel nurse, it helped to fill a void and need in my life.

Through the years, I have found that travel nurses are a special group of individuals. We usually travel alone; sometimes there are spouses, buddies, or pets, but the majority seems to travel by themselves. We pack our cars, trucks, and suitcases with those items that are near and dear to us. Maps or GPS systems mark our routes, or departure schedules lead the way. As a traveler, you find other travelers and become the tourist-explorer enjoying movie nights, bingo, line dancing, and nightly talks about joys and sorrows shared over bottles of wine. Travel nurses are not strangers to one another.

We find assignments off the beaten path or in major cities, and go because we are needed.

This story is fictional, about women who chose to leave their homes and go where they were needed, healing and learning, bonding and finding love along the way. The nurses in the Civil War were heroes, just like the women who disguised themselves and fought as men in many battles. The women who fought were given no recognition, and the status of soldiers was denied them during the Civil War. I am pleased there are many books now about these brave women who fought, held rank, and often died for their beliefs.

We should be proud of these women, nurses and soldiers, who forged the road for many of us to follow.

Acknowledgments

I need to thank some people who supported and encouraged me from the start of this project: Joan, Pat, Jackie, Jas, Nancy and Rosemarie. Thank you, ladies, for keeping me on the path and my eyes on the prize.

A Special thank you and standing ovation to the staff at Two Harbors Press who stepped in and made my dream come true. You are greatly appreciated.

Chapter 1
NEW YORK, AUGUST 1862

Franklin Alfred Prichard's hands permanently stained from the ink of the Franklin Weekly, after forty-five years had begun to resemble the brittle paper he read in his office. As the editor and owner, he looked over the articles written by one of his best reporters, Eric Samuel White Jr., or Samuel as he liked to be called. Franklin needed a few minutes away from the smell of ink and the sound of the printer finishing the weekly edition. He removed the black sleeve protectors from his arms and took his special bottle of bourbon from the bottom drawer of his desk. Its taste was always welcome, and it helped to make difficult decisions a little easier.

Samuel had come to work for the Weekly when he was eighteen. Franklin hired him as a favor to his old friend Eric White Sr., who felt his headstrong, unruly, and defiant son was headed for trouble and needed a proper lesson on the value of money. Eric attempted to be a mother and father to his four children after the death of his beloved wife, Eleanor. However, knowing the burden that Eric was dealing with at that time of his life—the issues with Samuel, two small daughters who needed a mother, and his other son, George, who was away at school—Franklin considered being asked to look after Samuel a reasonable request from an old friend.

Franklin started Samuel at the bottom at the Weekly. His twenty-year friendship with Eric afforded Samuel no favors. Eric owned one of the largest banks in New York, making him successful and wealthy even in wartime. He had loaned Franklin the money to start the Weekly, when no one else in the city would even give him an appointment to apply for a loan. He was forever in Eric's debt.

Samuel became interested in all aspects of the magazine, how the stories were written, printed, and then distributed, and he learned about the financial side of running a weekly magazine. After two years, Franklin allowed Samuel to go with a seasoned reporter to learn how to interview, hunt for the truth, and then put it into print. He proved to be a quick learner and seemed to have a flair for getting information from people. Franklin never imagined when the young man arrived on his doorstep how he would take to it. Eric had been oblivious to the change that had taken place with his son in the beginning, but he was now no longer ignorant of that fact. Franklin knew the future of the news business would involve taking risks. At twenty-four years old, Samuel, a likeable young man, took unnecessary chances to get a story.

Franklin laughed to himself recalling last November when Samuel posed as a waiter to obtain an exclusive interview with the attorney general-elect during the New York state election. Samuel snuck into the hotel suite with a bottle of liquor, made his introductions, and explained his purpose for being there. The attorney general should have thrown him out. Samuel should have been arrested, but instead the Weekly obtained the only personal interview given that night, as well as a private interview with the secretary of state-elect.

Samuel had a better grasp of how to sell a news story than men who had worked most of their lives in the business. Franklin saw in Samuel the same impressive talent and potential he had possessed at that age—half a lifetime ago. Franklin sat reading an outstanding report Samuel had written on the inauguration of President Lincoln on March 4, 1861. His next article in April of the same year on the surrender of Fort Sumter and what it could mean to the northern states was controversial. Samuel touched on the future cost of human lives, continued distrust between the North and South, and financial damage to the country. Samuel posed this question to his readers: "Why, as a nation, can we not settle our differences for all mankind?" Franklin took some criticism, public and private, for that article, but he was accustomed to complaints and, as the owner, was able to handle them without explanation or damage to the credibility of the Weekly.

Samuel's only problem now was his father.

What Eric had hoped would be a simple lesson for Samuel on the worth of money had turned into a career choice.

Franklin sighed and placed all of the articles back in the folder marked with Samuel's name. He poured himself another bourbon and leaned back in his chair. He had sent a reporter to the second battle at Bull Run. Samuel had made numerous requests to be sent with troops leaving New York every month. Franklin had refused up to this point, but he finally relented. Samuel would be sent to report on the battles between the states.

Franklin would send Samuel to war.

≈

THE WHITE MANSION
NOVEMBER 1862

The White mansion had been decorated for a pre-Thanksgiving gala. The chilling wind, crisp and cold, reminded Eric that winter approached.

Large fires warmed the main rooms where the guests would gather. The smell of turkey, cinnamon, and nutmeg filled every corner of the huge home. Surrounded by all the comforts his home provided, Eric couldn't relax. He watched as the servants scurried around finishing the last-minute touches while his wife, Julia, oversaw their work as she lounged on a chaise. Eric would have been happier if she had still been resting in bed rather than awake in a pale green morning wrapper that clung to her small bulge. This was the first time in two weeks that the twenty-eight-year-old had been allowed out of bed. Eric knew that Julia despised being so inactive, but he just couldn't allow the risk. This was their second pregnancy, and although he was overjoyed that Julia had made it to her sixth month, he could still not shake his anxiety and made Julia promise Dr. Daniel Develle that she would only direct the plans for today. Neither he nor Julia could bear to lose another child. Eric walked by and placed his hand on his wife's belly. The blessed kick was a reminder of the miracle growing inside her. Julia hoped this child would be a boy.

Dr. Develle, the family physician, had attended Eric's first wife, Eleanor, with the delivery of their children. Eleanor died eight years ago after delivering Emily. Eric married Julia four years later, when his other daughter, Ellen, was eight and Emily was four. Eric's son George was sixteen and away at school, and Samuel was working at the Franklin Weekly. Eric felt his daughters needed a mother. He could not be all they needed or would need in the years to come. There had been whispers in their community when Eric married someone half his age, but Eric and Julia fell in love with each other the first time they met, the first time he took her in his arms to dance.

Eric had discovered that his tall good looks, his black hair with slightly graying temples, and his sky-blue eyes possessed the ability to control a room. He had mesmerized her, just as he had been taken by her beauty. She came from a wealthy family, so money was never an issue. They were married within the year.

Julia smiled at Eric across the room and touched her stomach to indicate that the baby was kicking again. The servants quickly finished the last-minute details for the night's festivities. She went toward the downstairs guest room that had become the master bedroom until the baby arrived. Eric was relieved to see her keep her promise to Dr. Develle and rest.

~

A couple of hours before the party was set to begin, Eric sat in his library wearing his white shirt and black vest and listened to Julia's final directions to the servants. He had stripped off his stiff collar and tie, and relished in the one activity that relaxed him—looking over the household expenses, including the wrapper Julia had made especially for tonight. He smiled thinking of his pregnant wife giving orders instead of personally attending to the finer details. *I pray that this baby will come on time and that she will have no further problems. God, I love her so much that m y heart aches.*

Julia was completely different in every way from Eleanor: smaller—only five feet, five inches—with reddish blonde hair and green eyes that reminded him of summer grass. She had no interest in Eric's business. She loved their home and attended to its details. Before this pregnancy, Julia had spent most of her time outside in the gardens. Eric knew that being on bed rest had been difficult on his busy bee.

Eleanor, on the other hand, had been tall—close to six feet—with long, flowing dark brown hair and brown eyes. She had worked hard when they first arrived in New York. She had been more interested in their business and felt the servants could deal with managing the home.

Samuel had been born in the first year of their marriage. Eric struggled with opening the bank and being a husband and new father. Those first years were difficult, but they had managed. Eric credited Eleanor in many ways for the success of the bank. She could charm and entertain and had the ability to talk with respect in a man's world, Eric remembered. When she died, a part of me did, too. I felt there would never be another woman in my life. Julia changed all that for me. She breathed life back into my world, something I needed desperately.

Samuel had always reminded Eric of Eleanor the most, which might have been the reason he had been so hard on him, demanding more of his oldest son. Eleanor and Samuel had the same drive and determination toward things they wanted, and Eric worried that Samuel's defiance could seriously jeopardize his future plans with Atwood Pheleps. Atwood was an influential businessman, who had invited Eric to join his import-export business. I believe another lesson in life is necessary. We must all make sacrifices for family.

Eric's plans for his oldest son did not include him running all over the country writing about war for Franklin Prichard. The war between the states had been the opportunity that Atwood lived for; the smell of money to be made would be great for both men. At fifty years of age, Atwood, a large man who enjoyed his cigars and expensive brandy, had a daughter, Louisa Caroline. The lovely twenty-year-old was educated, and had been raised with all the privilege that wealth could offer. Louisa had been seriously interested in Samuel for about a year. A possible marriage will be an advantage to both families, with the progression of the war. Louisa had said many times, "Keep money with money."

Samuel had shown some interest in Louisa, but her snobbish attitude and lack of compassion had caused many a night to end in disaster—arguments with Louisa, her father, or her friends.

I'm hoping tonight will not be another mishap—too much is at stake. I am not happy with Atwood's policies at times, but the man is successful, and an alliance will assure a stronger legacy for my family.

∽

FRANKLIN WEEKLY

Samuel sat in Franklin Prichard's office. He dreaded the thought of spending hours with his father's friends, listening to boring conversations. He stood and stretched his tall frame. The constant twitter of Louisa and her social-climbing group of bitches will be more than I or any human should be subjected to. Louisa's father, Atwood Phelps, money-grubbing opportunist who sought to increase his empire off the backs of soldiers fighting in the war, always stunk of cigars and expensive brandy. Samuel didn't like him and trusted him even less. There were questions into the death of Atwood's wife that still needed to be addressed to Samuel's satisfaction. Samuel knew that Louisa and her father hoped she would marry Samuel and combine the empires of the Whites and Phelepses, but it would only be a marriage that was profitable on paper. Samuel didn't love her and knew he never would. The only person in the house that he could truly talk with would be Franklin, and possibly his brother George. George and Katherine had a new baby and had moved away from all the pomp and circumstance of New York. The chances they would come home were slight, but he hoped they would change their minds and bring his niece, Eleanor.

Samuel turned to see Franklin put on his dress jacket, took a quick look in the wardrobe mirror in the office, and ran his hand through his hair. Samuel watched as strands fell from the top of his head. "Where does all the time go?" Franklin said out loud, although Samuel was fairly certain the words were not directed to him. Franklin's only love had been the *Weekly*, and that left no time for marriage or a family. The Whites had been the only family Franklin had known. Franklin had always been more like a father than a boss.

Franklin sat down behind the desk.

"You look pretty good there, sir," Samuel said.

Franklin smiled. "You're planning to change when you get home, right? Your father will have a heart attack if you sit down to dinner dressed in work clothes."

Samuel looked at his brown plaid shirt, braces, and homespun pants.

"I am wearing my good clothes," Samuel said, and they both laughed.

Franklin pulled his favorite bottle of bourbon from the bottom drawer of the desk, along with two glasses.

"Samuel...," Franklin started. "I have something here that I think you will be interested in writing about. But you'll have to leave tomorrow and meet up with the Union troops heading toward Fredericksburg, Virginia."

Samuel was stunned. He didn't say anything for a minute. "Thanks, Franklin. I know this was not an easy decision for you, especially being so close to my father."

"Well, don't thank me yet. We still have a long evening to get through," Franklin said as he poured both of them a drink. "Atwood and his daughter are ruthless enough to surround the mansion with Union soldiers if they think you are going to leave," he laughed. "Let's drink to your health and a safe journey. All the information you'll need on returning your stories, couriers, personal contacts, and money is there."

Each man raised his glass and drank to health, safe travels, and a merciful night.

∽

The White Mansion
The Pre-Thanksgiving Gala

Samuel took the long way home after leaving work to think about the days ahead of him. Eric Samuel White Jr., war correspondent for the *Franklin Weekly*. It had a nice sound to it.

He arrived home to find early drinks being served in the main sitting room and immediately knew he was late. The finery in clothing and jewelry on the women repulsed him, especially when compared with all the horrors of war he had been reading about in the reports arriving daily at the Weekly. These people of prominence were isolated rather than ignorant of what was going on with the war, or just chose not to address the issues that did not immediately affect them. How can I continue to live with so much while others suffer and die?

His father's face was red and stern, a look Samuel had grown accustomed to these past few months. Franklin moved into Eric's view, no doubt attempting to distract his friend and save Samuel from conflict. Samuel heard Franklin ask about war loans and his possible business ventures with Atwood.

Julia met Samuel in the hallway, smiled, and handed him a letter, which brought an uncontrollable smile to his face. It was from Sarah, a family friend and someone he had come to count on after the death of his mother. Samuel thought about the first letter he had received from a fourteen-year-old girl that expressed her sympathy for his loss. He knew their families had a history but had not taken the time to learn what the history was. Samuel returned a note out of duty and respect for her family and did not expect to hear further from Sarah. She had surprised him a few months later with another letter. Over the next six years, Samuel had observed her grow into an intelligent, compassionate woman through their correspondence. He regretted the harsh letters about his father and family situation, but found she seemed to understand his anger and frustration. When Sarah's letter arrived announcing the death of her parents, Samuel wished he could have been there to wrap a supportive arm around her. He had hoped for a meeting, but with his assignment and the war, it would have to wait.

Samuel thought Julia looked stunning in the dark brown taffeta wrapper she had made for tonight. She wore the small diamond brooch that his father had given her for their anniversary that year.

"You're late," she teased. "Your clothes are on the bed. Hurry, please. I will hold dinner until you return."

Samuel leaned down, kissed her cheek, and said, "I'll be back shortly. Thank you."

Julia and Samuel had become friends. His feelings of resentment had slowly dissolved when she lost her first baby, and he decided that what she brought to the family was worth keeping.

As Samuel properly dressed, he was thankful this was the last time he would need formal clothing. He would no longer be subjected to these social gatherings of rich and boring individuals. He combed his thick brown hair, smiled, and went downstairs to join the masses.

In the main room, he was delighted to see Katherine, who handed him baby Eleanor for a quick hug and kiss.

George walked up and shook his hand. "I hear you will be leaving New York very soon."

Samuel looked surprised.

"Franklin told me," George said. "I promise it will be our secret until later."

"Thank you, brother. I am finally going to do what I really want with my life. I am going to go report all that I see and experience," Samuel proudly stated.

Samuel looked into Julia's eyes, and she smiled and gave a nodding approval to his appearance. She commanded the room as the lady of the house, took her husband's arm, and announced that it was time to be seated for dinner.

Entering the dining room, Samuel was assaulted by Louisa, dressed in a pink dress covered with huge bows which Samuel found hideous. Samuel figured that the necklace and earrings she wore could finance the entire war effort. I think I'll contact President Lincoln and advise him, Samuel mused.

"Samuel, I have saved a place for you," Louisa said as she pointed to the chair between herself and Atwood.

Samuel had seen this expression before and the ridiculous batting of her eyelashes. He would not give in to her childish games tonight.

"No, thank you, Louisa. I'm planning on actually enjoying my dinner tonight. Sitting with you would only sour whatever I put in my mouth," Samuel told her.

Louisa, shocked and embarrassed by his response, quickly looked to her father for help.

"Come now, Samuel," Atwood said. "We are all friends here."

"Some of us sitting at this table are friends, sir. Tonight I will sit with my family."

Samuel heard Franklin snicker as he quickly took Samuel's place between Atwood and Louisa. He will only need to endure their arrogance for m y sake this one last time.

Samuel found George and Katherine and sat down. He had a feeling of warmth tonight that had been absent for a long time where his family had been involved. Samuel found it strange to finally have something he'd longed and hoped for since his mother died. Tomorrow I will leave it behind.

Samuel passed off his feelings as assignment jitters. Dinner remained pleasant and conversation light. Father and Julia seemed to have accomplished what they intended—a few hours without the talk or thought of war. There were no arguments over Samuel's future at the dinner table. He knew that would come after dinner when the men would take their brandy into the library for talk not suited for women. The conversation would undoubtedly turn to his work at the Weekly. The women would adjourn to the sitting room for tea, dessert, and more twitter.

As the last of the dishes were removed by the servants, Father stood at the head of the table. "Gentlemen, there will be brandy and cigars waiting in the library. Shall we?"

Like obediently herded sheep, all the men stood to leave, including Samuel. Father had always been able to command and men would follow.

Leaving the dining room, Samuel heard Louisa's shrill voice telling the other women about the newest fashions from Paris and the dress she had ordered for the Union Christmas Ball.

His mind wandered for a moment. Will I ever meet a woman who can think for herself, a woman who converses equally with men and is not interested in my money? That type of woman would be challenging and intriguing. Samuel's thoughts settled on his childhood friend he had only known through letters.

The doors to the library seemed larger to Samuel tonight. Father's collection of books continually grew every year. Samuel found the fire inviting as he sat with a snifter of brandy in a large high-backed leather chair and watched the rest gather around him. Some sat, while others stood, but Samuel was the focus in the library tonight.

Atwood walked over to the fireplace, took a small piece of kindling, lit his cigar, and took a sip of his brandy, each movement precise, thoughtful, like a snake slowly uncoiling, preparing to strike. "Eric, my man, do you not think it's about time your oldest son settles down? He should start a family of his own and join our little adventure and prosper in New York society." Atwood's voice was loud and annoying.

"Atwood," Franklin started, "Samuel is not a child. He can make his own decisions about his life. Who are we to make life decisions for another man?"

"Son, I see no future in this hobby that Franklin has you playing," Eric said.

Franklin's brow rose at the comment from his old friend, and a hurt Samuel had not seen before settled on Franklin's face.

Eric continued. "My intentions were to teach you about the value of money, not have you waste your life on some dream of being a reporter."

"Eric, you feel I have wasted my life?" Franklin asked, walking over to face his friend. The conversation became intense. Samuel resisted the urge to interject into the argument brewing, supposedly for his sake, which increasingly seemed to have less and less to do with him. "I seem to remember it was you who insisted I follow my dream and start the Franklin Weekly," Franklin said. "I believe it was you who gave me the loan to start my business when no one else would help me. You did this to patronize me?"

Many of the men in the room backed away, giving space to the two men who stood like two boxers sparring in the ring. Samuel looked at his father's face and observed a redness rising above his stiff collar.

"No, no, old friend, please forgive me," Eric said. "I did not mean to say your life is wasted. I have always believed in you and your dream, but I do not want that for my son. I do not want him working for someone else. It seems my lesson in life has backfired on me, and I have created something that I can no longer control." Samuel prepared himself as his father finally turned to face him.

"Samuel, I want you to think about your future—a future working at the bank. Follow in my footsteps and take over management when I am no longer here." Father was sincere, almost pleading. Samuel knew his father had a point. Taking over the bank was his birthright—he was the oldest. George has just started a family and was too rural-minded for banking. Ellen and Emily, no matter what kind of women they grew to be, would always be out of the question. His youngest sibling had not yet been born, and Father wasn't getting any younger. It could have been a compelling argument if Samuel had been interesting in living someone else's life.

Before Samuel could reply, Franklin laughed. "My friend, I think you will be around for a while longer, especially with a new baby on the way and such a lovely wife who needs you."

There was agreement from the other men in the room, and glasses raised.

Atwood slithered next to Samuel's chair, spewing cigar smoke through this mouth and nostrils. He began his offer like an auction, and Samuel was for sale.

"Samuel, my boy, you have a wonderful opportunity here—money, status in the New York community, power, and a marriage to my lovely daughter. This will be a wonderful way to solidify our families."

Samuel knew what Atwood really meant. A marriage between Samuel and his daughter would result in the Phelepses becoming richer and more powerful than they already were at the present. Samuel remained silent.

"What do you say? Speak up, boy," Atwood laughed nervously. "This is the offer of a lifetime. You only stand to gain. I'm the only one sacrificing here. Weddings are extravagant and costly with flowers, food, liquor, a ridiculously expensive white dress, and possibly thousands of invitations. I'm the one losing out here, but I'm willing to do it for you, son."

Atwood's speech had nauseated Samuel. He was aware that money and power were the only things of interest to Atwood, who finished off his brandy in a large gulp, and then used his hand to wipe away what had not made it to his mouth. Samuel knew Atwood's self-serving nature. He imagined the man's thoughts congregating with images of the most powerful people his new wealth would soon be able to buy—senators, governors, and possibly the attorney general—power. And if all those powerful men come...how could President Lincoln refuse his influence? He has numerous contracts with the government. How could anyone say no? In the end, power, absolute power, would be worth any cost to Atwood.

Samuel watched as Atwood tried to maintain his composure and excitement as he continued his sale. "We can arrange a Christmas wedding and a honeymoon away from all the violence and bloodshed. What do you say, my man? Will you become a son to me?" Atwood grinned, believing he could never be refused.

Samuel sat quietly, listening to the insanity. Finally, he stood and faced the room, full of his father's so-called friends. He watched Franklin back up to the wall and smile. George nodded his head toward him, silently saying, Go ahead, you can do this.

Atwood's continuously reddening face amused Samuel. He knew Atwood was waiting for him to take the foul bait that had been thrown out. Samuel knew many of the men in the library believed Samuel would not refuse and would have taken the offer themselves if given the chance. Samuel could feel the tension in the room tightening around him like a rope around the neck of the condemned.

"Father, I want to thank you for sending me to Franklin six years ago," Samuel began. "He gave me direction when I had none. At the time, I was frustrated with you, and I could not accept Mother's death. I acted in the only way I knew how—with anger and defiance. Franklin took all that anger and showed me another place for it. I have discovered a job, a career, that I love and enjoy with all my heart. I have a passion that seems to grow every day. I could never work at the bank with you." Samuel looked at Atwood and could see that his breathing had increased.

Samuel continued, "There is no desire, no passion there for me. I do not seek more money, power, or an arranged marriage to a woman I do not, and will never, love."

Atwood reached for his collar to loosen it, releasing a bead of sweat that ran from his face down his shirt.

Straightening his jacket, Samuel turned, faced Atwood, and cleared his throat.

"Mr. Pheleps, I would rather kiss the back end of a Confederate mule than be married to your social-climbing, insensitive, uncaring snob of a daughter."

Atwood reached out for the wall to steady his stance.

"There will be no Christmas wedding. I am leaving tomorrow on assignment for the Weekly."

Franklin, George, and several other men applauded.

Eric walked over to his son. "I do not approve of the profession you have chosen. But when you stand and speak as a man of your convictions, it demands my respect."

Atwood dropped his drink and opened his mouth to speak, but no words formed. He fell to the floor and had to be helped to his seat.

Samuel assumed he was in shock. I know no man has ever stood up to that fat bastard before.

"Now gentlemen, if you will excuse me, I have to pack. Father, I will see you and Julia in the morning. I wish to spend time privately with the family before I leave New York." Samuel left the library. He had a feeling of freedom he had never known until that moment.

Samuel returned to his room and removed the letter from the inside pocket of his dinner jacket. While the letter may have merely been from a childhood friend, to Samuel they were the words of someone who had always understood, never judged, and continued to support him. He savored the quiet and each word of the letter from Sarah.

Dear Samuel,

I hope this finds you well. Many things have happened since I received your last letter...

∾

The Cover of the Franklin Weekly, two days after Samuel left for Fredericksburg.

Special Edition.

Atwood Pheleps, fifty, import-export mogul, dies in his sleep, cause unknown. Survived by one daughter, Louisa, who has left New York for Paris to mourn her father's death.

∾

Pheleps shipping was bought by Eric White at the agreed price should either die, a partnership signed at Atwood's insistence the day of the party.

Chapter 2

A small fire burned in a stove in a shed behind the Albany Baptist Church, where a tiny figure huddled to stay warm. There was no snow, just a cooler breeze than Mack expected.

Mack was from Pearlington, Mississippi, and during her eighteen years of life, she had fished and hunted this time of year in just a smidgen of a shirt and short pants. This fire was a welcome sight. Mack remembered what her maw always told her and her brothers: If you is ever away from home, hungry, lost, or cold, church folks is the closest thing to family. I never known church folks to turn those in need away.

Mack, or Martha Ann Catherine Keens, found that to be true this day. She arrived in Albany in time for the two-hour Sunday sermon and noticed that the good folks there were friendly to a young boy who was in need of hot food and clean and warmer clothes. One of the church ladies offered to fill a barrel full of hot water and get the new soap she'd bought in Macon. The church lady said the soap was intended to get a person clean and close to God. Mack thanked her and said, "I've been kinda poorly and will get close to God next Sunday."

She was warm now; her belly full of good Christian cooking and covered with a quilt that didn't have any holes in it. The clothes they brought her were a little short, but they'd do. The britches had a flap front with buttons. Mack was use to tie pants, and the shirt was made from soft material and warm. The boots were a little big, so they brought two sets of socks. Life was good, and she even had food for the morning. The preacher and his wife tried to get Mack to stay at their home, but Mack told them, "This here shed is good enough." It had a door that was tight and the wind didn't blow through the boards. All the church ladies brought extra covers for her to make a bed, and there was clean straw, too. Mack knew everything would be just fine.

Mack didn't correct the church ladies about her not being a boy. Mack's maw had wanted three girls, but what she had was seven boys and Mack, so Mack had all three names to carry. Since she was the last to be born, boys' clothes was what she wore, except for the Sunday-go-to-meeting dress. Mack knew she was small, just a bit more than halfway up the inside of the door where everyone got marked at home. Pa said, "That girl don't weigh nothing" She had crawled up on the feed-weigher down at Mr. Howard's feed store. All she remembered was at the beginning of planting season this year, a big bag of feed was heavier than her.

The one thing that bothered Mack was not finishing school, because that was important now that she was headed to help the boys in gray. She needed to be able to read if she was going to be a spy. Most of her brothers had gone toward New Orleans to join up and fight.

Mack's memory served her well when it came to people and places. She never got lost if people gave the right directions. She was always in trouble with her brothers for suddenly appearing when she was not wanted or needed. She kept her raven black hair cut inappropriately short for a girl, but short hair suited her. Her eyes almost matched her hair and her tanned skin was beautiful, but not soft, and could be mistaken for handsome rather than pretty. Mack carried a knife and could use it better than all of her brothers back home. Mack could see at night like it was day, and tended to borrow what was needed along the way to help her get from place to place. This ability assisted Mack on her journey to Albany without coins in her pocket.

If she hadn't fallen in the river trying to get a fish for dinner, she would have been good enough to get to Waynesboro. The preacher told Mack that Waynesboro was still a good seven to ten days of walking unless he caught a ride somewhere along the way.

Mack was on a mission to get a letter from a boy named Ethan Raymond Bowen, a year younger than herself, to his sister. He and some of his friends were heading to a place called Galveston, Texas. They were going to go join the fight there.

They had come through Pearlington and stopped at the house needing food and such.

Maw told them they could stay and that she didn't have much, but she would share what we had been given by the good Lord above. That was the beginning of summer. Just before Ethan and the other boys left, he asked Mack to keep a letter for his sister and maybe pass it on to anyone going toward Georgia.

Ethan told her that he had made a promise to write his sister and let her know he was alive and well. She told him she'd do what she could; it wasn't right to worry family. Mack asked Ethan how he had learned to read and write so "good." Ethan explained to her that his mother had taught all of the children to read and write properly. He said they had school in the kitchen every day. Chores were always done after lessons. His mother and father believed education was the most important thing parents could give them. When they died, his sister, Sarah, took over instructing him until he left home.

That very night, Mack made a spit-in-the-dirt, blood-brother oath to get that letter to his sister. In the morning light Mack would keep her oath, and in a few days, she'd get that letter to Sarah Jane Bowen of Waynesboro, Georgia.

Chapter 3

FREDERICKSBURG, VIRGINIA
DECEMBER 11-15, 1862

Samuel was trying to warm up after another cold night in his tent. He was thankful that he had read all of the information Franklin had given him before leaving New York. The extra blanket, heavier coat, and sweater he had brought with him had proved to be useful. The letters and suggestions from the other reporters about preparing as much as possible for the unknown weather conditions had been helpful, but nothing could really prepare anyone for the actuality of war.

Samuel assimilated quickly, gathering names and collecting favors from enlisted men, promising to send their letters back home with his story about the upcoming battle. However, standing outside Major General Ambrose E. Burnside's tent had almost gotten him sent packing back to New York on more than one occasion since his arrival. Samuel was not used to being put off by people when it came to getting information for a story. The first lieutenant outside the general's tent was easy pickings after Samuel offered him the fresh tobacco he had brought for leverage. There was a lot of activity involved in preparing pontoon bridges, which were to be placed over the Rappahannock River so that troops could enter Fredericksburg as well as position men and armaments. Samuel needed more information, and the first lieutenant was more than happy to trade secrets for tobacco, a happy coincidence which procured Samuel access to the battlefield for a more accurate story.

While the other reporters sat around the fire drinking coffee and smoking, Samuel walked out to look at the battlegrounds. The sea of blue uniforms made the ground look like water.

"There's not a lot to look at right now, sir." The small voice startled Samuel.

Samuel looks down to see a child in Union clothing speaking to him.

"And you are?" Samuel smiled and wondered what business this child had on a battlefield.

"Nathan Henry Jackson, drummer, Army of the Potomac, sir." The boy spoke with the pride of an adult.

"How old are you?" Samuel asked.

"Eleven, sir. I'll be twelve next week," Nathan answered proudly.

Before Samuel could ask any more questions, the boy was called away by a sergeant. My God, he's the same age as my sister Ellen. The thought of that young boy being in battle, possibly dying, sent a chill down his back. Samuel thought he was prepared to handle death and observe the injuries that war would bring, but that was for men, not boys. Samuel looked to see not only Nathan, but several young boys now preparing for the battle when they should have been playing marbles at school recess. He snapped back to the present when the sound of gunfire and artillery shells began. It was time to do what he was sent to do: report.

Samuel dug in with the rest of the troops. He wrote about what he saw and did not waver when Union troops looted the city. The truth needs to be reported. Over the course of two days, Union soldiers were deployed in preparation for the main battle.

∽

On December 14th, after continuous defeats by Confederate troops, Samuel could not imagine how this battle would ever be won. He spent a long night listening to the screaming and crying of men dying on the battlefield. The time spent in the surgery observing soldier after soldier being brought in to be saved was staggering.

What impressed and enlightened Samuel over the course of the night were the nurses who never wavered from their assigned duties. He watched as they bandaged and cared for dying men, holding their hands and then going to the next man screaming for help.

Samuel wondered if this scene was being played out across the river. Are there women tending to the Confederate men too? Was the horror there as bad as what he had seen here?

Thoughts drifted back to the article he had written over a year ago attempting to make people understand exactly what he had been afraid would happen—death to the American people at the hands of Americans. No foreign enemy here, just brothers killing brothers.

Samuel sat down on the ground for a moment and took out the unfinished letter to Sarah he had started before leaving New York. After watching the nurses attending to the injured, he thought about how many times Sarah wrote to him about her healing practices with nature. Although he had never met her, Samuel wondered if she was the type of woman that would become involved in this war to heal the injured.

Sarah,

I have been sent to write about the war and all who serve. I now realize this must include women, nurses who care for the sick and dying. I hope you will remain safe and away from these horrors. My letters may become farther apart, but I will try to find a way to keep in contact.

Your friend,

Samuel

Samuel placed the letter in his pocket so it would not mix in with the letters he had promised to send back to soldiers' families. He walked over to Burnside's tent, listening to generals and subordinates arguing and pleading with Major General Burnside to stop the fighting. Their men were wounded and needed attention. Confederate sniper fire made it impossible to help those in need. Plans for another attack were made, but later in the day, a letter was sent to General Lee asking for a truce so the wounded could be attended.

That request was granted.

On December 15th, federal forces retreated across the river and the campaign ended.

Samuel finished his report with the following: Union casualties 12,653. The deaths of Brigadier Generals George D. Bayard and Conrad F. Jackson were only two more in a long line of special men that would never make it home.

On the morning of the 16th, Samuel packed his things to leave, then walked to surgery. He once again looked at the injured and dying men who were being attended to by nurses. These nurses would travel across the land to care for those who call upon them.

This is a story that will be told, must be told to the rest of the nation. The women of war, who are they, why are they here? Samuel looked up and saw Joseph Bines, a courier for the Weekly, waiting for him. Franklin did not trust wire service and wanted Samuel's handwritten stories and personal notes.

"Tell me all about this battle. What was it like?" Joseph asks.

"It's not what everyone thinks. This is not a game, and if we are not careful, we will lose everything that is dear." Before Samuel could finish, he saw the body of Nathan Henry Jackson, soon to be twelve, stacked with the rest of the dead like wood.

Samuel turned and vomited on his boots, and wiping the tears away before Joseph noticed.

Trying to compose himself, he handed a package to Joseph, which included all the letters from soldiers he promised would be sent back to their families. He would never truly know how many of those men died. His letter to Sarah was given to Joseph separately with instructions for delivery.

Climbing on his horse, Samuel left with the rest of the troops, away from Fredericksburg.

Chapter 4

BOWEN FARM
DECEMBER 16, 1862
WAYNESBORO, GEORGIA

Sarah Jane Bowen had lived on the Bowen Farm since she was three years old, almost seventeen years ago. She sat in the cold root cellar reading Samuel Thomson's New Guide to Health; or Botanic Family Physician, published 1835, by dim lantern light. The book had belonged to Elise Bowen, a gift from her friend Eleanor. James Frank Bowen, called Frank by the men he worked with, had come to the granite quarry as a young man to work. Once he married and children appeared, he wanted a life close to family. His brother had land in Georgia, and the offer to work in the sunshine appealed to Frank. Elise Bowen, his wife, was a healer and midwife who was taught in another part of the world. She was educated, intelligent, and made her way to America where Frank met and married her. James and Sarah were born before the Bowens moved to Waynesboro. Ethan made his appearance two years after they settled into farm life.

Sarah checked the book to make sure the flowers and roots were being preserved correctly and no mold was growing on them. Sarah knew her mother would have been upset if anything was ruined due to her inability to follow the rules. Sarah found the book so interesting she read it daily. She had a wonderful herb garden and planned on another if she and James were still on the farm. The war had made so many decisions difficult these days.

Elise had her own book for healing, keeping separate pages on every ailment from fevers, broken bones, pain remedies, coughs, colic, childbirth medications—too many to memorize—and had cross-referenced them with the book Sarah was reading. "I will never be the healer mother was," she said out loud to no one. She touched the heart necklace that lay gently around her neck.

It was a constant reminder that the people we love could leave all too soon. The necklace had belonged to her mother, a gift on a first wedding anniversary from a man that loved his wife more than life itself. Frank cut the rose quartz heart by hand and placed it in a simple setting, symbolizing his love always for his beloved Elise.

Frank and Elise were returning from Augusta two years ago with supplies. There was a spring storm; lightning spooked the horses. The wagon overturned, killing Elise instantly. Frank was seriously injured and died within the month, more of grief than of his injuries. Elise's necklace now belonged heart and soul to Sarah.

Sarah continued reading about marshmallow plant, thyme, onion, garlic, and meadowsweet herb; these all have healing properties, and some decrease swelling. Skullcap, rosemary, chamomile, and black cherry have a sedative and calming ability. Sarah tried to see how they could be prepared and saved for travel. There were many herbs, flowers, plants that grew so readily in nature that procuring and saving would not be necessary. Sarah's ability to recognize them might have been an issue, especially in an area not familiar to her. She thought about the herbs she had in the warming cupboard and realized how much time had passed in the cellar. She picked up a small container of carrier oil made from sunflowers. There were several jars of scented water that needed to be strained in a few days. She loved to use them to scent bathwater. Christmas was only nine days away, food to be cooked, housecleaning for overnight company, laundry, and finishing the dress she had made for this year's holiday. I have too much to do and need some help.

～

James Bowen walked through the house, adjusting his braces and looking for Sarah. She was never where he could find her. James saw a letter on the kitchen table addressed to Sarah. It was six months old and from Samuel White. James recalled the story his father had told him of a poor young boy who saved the life of a wealthy, spoiled young man. That young man was Eric White. Eric had been sent to the quarry to learn the lesson of hard work. Frank and Eric's friendship began that day in the quarry before marriages, children, and new lives away from Connecticut. James remembered his father telling the children how two beautiful women, who were friends later, charmed those two young men. The families remained in contact until Eleanor's death. The death of Eleanor White had drawn Samuel and Sarah together. In the beginning, they wrote to honor the memory of family; now he wasn't sure. This was Sarah's business, not his. James put the letter back and walked to the back door, looking toward the barn and root cellar. He walked out of the house and began to yell.

"Sarah? Sarah, where are you? We have company," James yelled.

James had been watching a tiny figure walk toward the farm for the last twenty minutes.

This boy finally walked through the gate where James could see he was covered with some type of rash. He kept asking for Sarah.

"Can I help you, young man?" James asked.

"No, sir, I needs to find Sarah Jane Bowen of Waynesboro. It's a sum importance I talk with her," the young boy said firmly.

Since Sarah was the local healer and many people came to see her, James assumed this young man needed medical attention. Sarah was probably in the root cellar as that seemed to be where she spent more and more time. After the war started, Sarah had been making more lotions, poultices, creams, drying flowers, and gathering herbs than she normally did this late in the year. He worried about his sister since Ethan left. Many women in their community had left to go find the men they loved and help in the fight.

Sarah would leave to heal.

⌒

Sarah walked out of the cellar dusting dirt from her brown day wrapper. "James, why are you screaming?" Sarah asked. As she reached the house, she touched her shoulder. "I guess I left it in the cellar," she said to James.

"Your shawl is in the house," James said.

The shawl belonged to Elise, and it was special to Sarah. It made her feel close to her mother.

"Hurry, you have to see this," James told her.

"What?" Sara said.

"Not what but who. It's a young boy, and he is asking for you."

Sarah was surprised to see what appeared to be a boy about the age of thirteen standing in their home. He was dirty, with torn clothes, and scratching everywhere, trying to hand her a piece of paper.

"Lord God almighty, excuse me, ma'am, but you sure does look like your brother Ethan," He told Sarah.

When Sarah realized that the boy had seen Ethan, she grabbed the piece of paper and sat down to read it.

Sarah could tell from James's fidgeting that he was more worried about what the boy had brought into the house and if it was catching. Tears began to well in Sarah's eyes as she read the letter out loud to James.

Sis,

I am keeping the promise I made to you when I left last April. Please let everyone know that we are in Pearlington, Mississippi, and have had no injuries or misfortunes. Thanks to the Keens, we are warm and well fed. It will take another month to get to Galveston, due to heavy fighting in the southern part of Louisiana; hopefully, we can catch a ship and make better time. Tell James I am sorry, but I had to do this. We all have to take a stand in this war, and this is mine. I will write again.

I hope you will remain well and safe until this war has ended and we are together as a family again.

Your brother,

E.

Sarah cried holding the letter. She reached for the boy saying, "Thank you, thank you." James watched as he backed away from Sarah's touch, probably due to the rash.

"Ma'am, it weren't nothing. Please don't cry. He and them other fellows are just fine," He said. "I was a worried about finding you. Them last two fellows I got information from was not true, and I was not sure I'd know you, but that yellow hair and blue eyes match Ethan's. Ethan was a lot taller than him," the boy finished pointing to James.

"Ethan grew past James when he was sixteen," Sarah said.

James huffed. He was not sure about the young boy. There seemed to be something not right, but he couldn't figure it out at the moment.

"Ethan felt the need to leave and fight. He had always talked about the sea, ships, and being a pirate one day when he was a boy. I guess he will get the chance now to sail the sea," Sarah said, looking to James.

"Ethan should be back here helping us take care of the farm," James yelled. He was mad just thinking about how Ethan up and left in the middle of the night in late April, just as the tobacco needed to be topped and suckered. There was no telling how long Ethan had been planning it.

"I want you to stop this," Sarah said. "Enough is enough. We made it through just fine with the help from Uncle Mike."

Michael Bowen was their father's older brother. His tobacco farm dwarfed theirs, so there were always extra slaves who could be sent to them.

"All that matters is he is alive and well," Sarah said.

Sarah stopped and looked at this young boy who had traveled so far to bring a letter from someone he barely knew.

"Please forgive me. We have forgotten our manners. Will you stay and have dinner with us?" Sarah asked this young man.

"Thank you, ma'am. That would be mighty nice. My name is Mack Keens," he said, scratching.

Sarah finally looked at the terrible rash and said, "Come with me. I think I can fix this."

Mack smiled and Sarah took the young boy to the kitchen. She yelled to James to find one of his old shirts.

James stomped out of the main room to find clothes for this, this, well, he wasn't sure what Mack was.

⌒

Sarah filled a washtub with tepid water. "Mack, I am going to put some oats in the water to help with the rash. I don't want you to use any soap, just soak. I will wash your hair after you get out. Then when you're finished, I'll have James put a salve on you to help with the itching." Sarah rambled on in a fast manner.

"Ma'am, ma'am. He can't do that!" Mack said.

Sarah was perplexed. "Why not?" she asked.

"I ain't no boy. I is a girl, and the curse came upon me today. I is in a bad mess. Can you help me?" Mack begged Sarah.

"Absolutely," Sarah laughed.

"Please don't say nothing to your brother. I is ashamed. I don't want him knowing I is a girl just yet," Mack said.

"It will be our secret for now, I promise. James really doesn't get involved in my healing."

Sarah gathered chamomile for tea, honey from the cabinet, and clean rags for the curse. She put more wood in the stove to keep the kitchen warm. While Mack was soaking and water boiled for tea, Sarah took a leather glove and worked dried herbs in a circular motion so that the stems did not get crushed. There was still much to prepare and properly store, but it would have to wait until tomorrow. Sarah had asked for help in the cellar. Looking at Mack, she thought perhaps it had been sent in the form of this young child.

Mack didn't like the slimy feeling of the water, but the itch was better. Sarah washed Mack's hair and trimmed it so she would keep her boyish look.

"I thank you kindly, ma'am," Mack said.

Sarah smiled at her. She then gave Mack a bowl of soup and fresh bread. Mack devoured everything and asked for more.

Mack felt so lucky to be in the Bowens' home that night and not sleeping in that tree covered with what Sarah called poison oak. Mack was angry that she hadn't seen that vine when she climbed that tree to sleep in three nights ago. Sarah had made something she called a poultice that was warm and used for the curse pains. It was helping, and the cream made with some flowers called marigold had all but made the itching stop. She was a lucky girl tonight with a shirt that smelled good and clean under things. Sarah promised to send for clothes that fit in the morning.

"Mack, I want you to drink this so you'll sleep and not scratch during the night," Sarah insisted.

"This don't smell right, Miss Sarah," Mack snarled.

"I know, but I put honey in it. I promise you will sleep better—it's made from flowers called chamomile."

"Okay, but I have something to ask you."

"Tomorrow, Mack. Just rest. You can stay with us as long as you like, but first you have to get better."

Mack began to drink the tea; being tired and sick had taken a toll, but clean and in a warm bed, she quickly fell asleep. The last she felt was Sarah pulling the quilt around her shoulders. Sarah left after listening to Mack's steady, clear breathing, and the last that Mack heard was Sarah heading downstairs to face James. Mack thought there might be harsh words between brother and sister. James hadn't seemed happy that she was there, but she already felt close to Sarah and knew she would fight to let her stay.

∾

"Sarah, I want that boy gone," James started.

"I am not going to talk to you about this tonight, James. Mack needs to get over the poison oak and rest. My God, James, do you know where that child came from? How far Mack traveled to bring that letter to us?" Sarah said.

"There's something not right about him," James continued. "He's too young to be traveling alone. We can't take in people like stray animals. He has to go back home. The war, I mean, he has family right?" James rambled on.

"Mack will stay with us until I decide he is well enough to travel. That is the Christian thing to do for the gift he brought us today. Please don't bring this up again. We have more than enough room in this huge, empty home."

"Well, I guess I can find work around here for him. Not sure, since he is kind of small. I still need help with the late crop of tobacco we harvested. He can help me with the drying." James said. He knew he was not going to win this argument.

"Good, because I can use his help when you do not need him. I have a lot of work in the root cellar with my herbs," Sarah said. "Good night. And will you burn Mack's clothes? They are not salvageable." Sarah walked toward the stairs.

"Sarah," James quietly called to his sister. "It is nice to know Ethan is well. I miss him, too." He then headed out to check the animals in the barn before turning in for the night.

∽

The next morning Mack got up and began to put on clothes that were probably James's or Ethan's when they were a bit younger, and some shoes that really did fit with only one pair of socks. Mack even found a new cap. Sarah was good on her word to not leave a dress. She left clean boy's underwear and rags for the curse. The rash didn't look so mean, and her pains were not bad. Mack could smell bacon and coffee; she ran downstairs.

"Mornin', ma'am," Mack said.

"Call me Sarah." Sarah paused, contemplating her next question. "Tell me, how old are you? James and I were thinking thirteen or fourteen."

Mack laughed out loud."You ain't even close. I is a year older than your brother Ethan."

Sarah sat down at the table looking at this young woman in disbelief.

"I would never have believed you were more than a twig," she told Mack.

Mack poured syrup on her hotcakes, licked her fingers, and then reached for another piece of bacon. She felt now was the time to ask the favor. "Miss Sarah, can I ask you that favor now?"

"I will do anything within my power. For what you did for Ethan and our family, it will be a small price to pay."

"I want you to school me. I need to finish my reading and writing. I'm gonna be a spy for the South. I gots a good memory, and I'll try real hard. Ethan told me you was a good teacher. I'd be ever so thankful if you'd help me."

Sarah smiled and reached out to hug Mack. She had a feeling that this was the beginning of a friendship, one that both would learn from.

"How long can you stay?"

Chapter 5

NINE DAYS LATER
CHRISTMAS MORNING

Sarah was awakened by the smell of coffee and knew James had already started a fire to warm the kitchen for her. Sarah poured lilac water to wash. She combed and pinned her hair back so it would remain neat while she cooked. After dressing in her holiday dress that was finished just for this day, Sarah picked up a mirror and looked at her image. She sat down and thought of Samuel so far away. Sarah hoped one day they would meet and talk about all the years that have passed between them, to finally put a face with his name. Sarah put these thoughts away as today she would focus on family and her new friend.

As Sarah walked past Mack's room and headed downstairs, she thought about how Christmas was special that year because of Mack. Sarah had hope that their family would survive the war and come together again. Mack had been quite a surprise. She worked like a man in the morning with James and studied until she fell asleep at night. Sarah knew that judging someone due to the way they were raised or spoke was wrong. She was not sure Mack would succeed, although Mack was bright and learned quickly. Mack retained quite a bit of knowledge from her early years in school, which had helped Sarah accelerate the lessons.

It was unfortunate that many children were unable to finish their studies due to family hardships.

James had softened toward Mack. James had told Sarah the other evening that Mack was quite a hard worker for such a young boy. Sarah smiled remembering her promise—a promise she would keep until Mack decided to reveal her true self. Sarah planned to work with Mack on speech once her reading and writing improved. There would be some difficulty with the heavy Mississippi accent, but she believed she could minimize it. Sarah hoped that once Mack understood what she read, there would be time to teach her about nature. Mack had shown interest in its healing ability.

"Learning about what's in nature could help our boys in war, Miss Sarah," Mack said at dinner the previous evening.

The more questions Mack asked helped Sarah to prepare her for when she would leave the Bowen farm. The thought of Mack leaving saddened Sarah, but the determination of that young woman was not to be questioned. Sarah worried about Mack becoming a spy, but she knew Mack could take care of herself.

Sarah walked into the kitchen and poured a cup of coffee, then reached for her best apron and found the small gift in the warming cupboard she had been hiding for Mack. Sarah couldn't wait to see Mack's face when she gave her the small gift, just between friends. It was not new but something Sarah had enjoyed for years and felt that she should pass down for someone else to enjoy. She returned the gift to its hiding place.

～

There was a knock at the back door and there stood Rebecca and Agnes, two slaves that belonged to Uncle Mike. Sarah had them come inside due to the chill of the morning air.

"What are you two doing here this early?" Sarah asked, knowing Uncle Mike sent them.

"Miss Sarah," Rebecca started. "We comes to help you with the cookin'."

"I cannot believe he did this! It's Christmas!" Sarah was furious.

"Miss Sarah, don't be mad at Mista Mike. He knows you works so hard he wanted us ta help you." Agnes tried to calm Sarah.

"I will not have it!" Sarah said. "Rebecca, Agnes, come with me." Sarah poured coffee and took out fresh bread and jam. They said a quick prayer, ate, and Sarah gathered an extra ham, breads, eggs, and coffee to send back with them.

"Miss Sarah, we has some children that have a sickness," Rebecca told her.

"What type of illness?"

"Some of the children ain't eating and have a fever," Agnes replied.

"None of them has any spots and no coughs," Rebecca said.

Sarah grabbed some herbs and told Rebecca and Agnes how to prepare them. "If this does not work, you send Ben for me."

"We will Miss Sarah, God bless you."

"Now let me get James to take you two back," Sarah said.

"No ma'am, we has one of the smaller wagons and we can get back ourselves," Agnes said.

Sarah wrote a note to Uncle Mike chastising him for sending Agnes and Rebecca to the farm. She reminded him and Aunt Lilly to not be late for Christmas dinner. Sarah gave the note to Rebecca.

"You tell Uncle Mike that I will talk to him later about this." Sarah was still angry.

Agnes and Rebecca laughed. "I bet you will, Miss Sarah," Rebecca said.

They took what Sarah had given them and put it in the wagon.

Sarah stood and watched until they were on their way. She then went in and started cooking, something she knew would take her most of the day. Sarah hoped Ethan and his friends would find warmth and safety this day. What stories he will have when we see him again.

The Christmas meal was plentiful. Family and friends had been arriving at the Bowen farm since daybreak. Mack wore a black pair of homespun pants and a blue plaid shirt with braces. She blended in with the rest of the men, as more people came to the front door. She felt uneasy but stayed at Sarah's insistence.

"You have to feel comfortable in all of your surroundings, Mack." Sarah smiled. "You have fooled everyone. They all think you're a boy."

The music playing throughout the house was from men and women who brought their instruments. The warm scent of food filled every corner. There was laughter and smiles from everyone, which made her feel like family. Mack went outside with James to get more firewood for the overnight guests.

"Mack, you and I will be sleeping in the barn tonight with the rest of the men. The women are going to gaggle all night," James told her.

Mack looked at James while he handed her firewood. She noticed his tan had not faded with winter, and his six foot frame looked taller today. James wore his good brown homespun britches, a tan shirt with stripes, and his braces. She never noticed how his braces fit across his shoulders so well or how thick his brown hair was, never having seen him without a hat. She thought he looked very different. She searched in her mind for the word. Handsome.

"What did ya say? Sleep in the barn?" Mack's speech slipped whenever she was taken by surprise or worried.

"You don't want to stay inside with the women, do you?"James laughed. "You would never get any sleep."

God above, what am I a-gonna do now?

They went back into the house with the firewood. Mack walked into the kitchen and then into the main dining room. Mack had never seen so much food in her entire life.

Every woman came through the door carrying at least two bowls or pans of food for the main table. Mack had never asked James or Sarah why they had no slaves, especially with such a large farm, but this was not the day for that talk. Today, it was just good to be here with her new friends.

James called everyone to the table; children sat at a smaller table, but everyone was together.

"Shall we all join hands?" James asked everyone. "May the good Lord bless family and friends. Protect those away from the ones who love them. We thank you for the bounty you have given this day and for all that sit at this table. Amen."

Mack silently said a prayer for the family she left in Pearlington.

On Sarah's insistence, the women sat with the men, shared food, and talked. There was no hurry to go back to the fields. On this day, everyone shared what they had with those they loved.

Mack couldn't remember a day like this in her short life. Being the youngest, she always sat at the far end of the table. She rarely had any hot bread, and the meat had lots of fat on it, if there was meat at all. She was used to a lot of beans and taters. Mack not only got all the hot bread and butter she wanted but also meat, vegetables, gravy, and fresh honey that Uncle Earl brought from his bees.

After dinner, the music continued, people sang, and everyone danced, including Sarah. Mack was shown a table full of sweet things—pies, cakes, cobblers, candies—and was told to eat all she wanted by Aunt Lilly.

Mack went outside to drink coffee with the men who were smoking and chewing tobacco. Uncle Mike showed two jugs he had brought for the night's conversations in the barn. He swore this was some of his best home brew.

Sarah had made tea for the women. There was laughter and smiles on all the faces in the Bowen home.

It had been a good day, but night came all too soon. Mack was nervous about going out to the barn with the men.

"Mack, you'll be fine," Sarah smiled at her. "Just pretend they are your brothers."

"It's not the same."

"Well, unless you are ready to tell James and the others who you really are, I suggest you take this quilt and head outside."

"No, no, not yet. It's too soon. I is not ready. Miss Sarah, don't you be a-tellin' him yet." Mack started to panic. She realized she had mispronounced her words and was embarrassed.

"Fine, I'll see you and the rest of the men in the morning," Sarah laughed and pushed Mack out the back door.

Mack walked slowly to the barn, wishing it would go away or she could go away. She just didn't want to sleep in the barn with a bunch of men. Mack was forced to share everything with her brothers back home. She had enjoyed sleeping in a bed alone in clean sheets, brightly colored quilts, and a pillow full of feathers that smelled like fresh flowers. Mack remembered today was Christmas. It's only one night. What could be so bad about one night? As Mack entered the barn, she could hear laughing in the loft. The climb to the loft was like walking up a gallows.

"Mack, Mack over here," James said, as she climbed over the ladder.

Mack slowly walked over to where James and several of the men were making pallets with hay and quilts. Mack put on an extra shirt to help stay warm and aid in her disguise.

"I cannot understand what women have to talk about after a full day of talking," James told the crowd of men.

The other men laughed and continued to make their beds of hay.

"One day you will, James," Uncle Mike said. "Women never run out of something to say, even if it's about nothing."

What Mack thought would be a night where the men would just go to sleep turned into continuous laughing, loud talk, belching, passing gas, and passing the jug. They talked about the war, the wins and losses, and whether James would join the battle.

Uncle Earl asked James, "Have you heard from Ethan? Is he well?"

"Mack, tell everyone about Ethan," James said.

Mack sighed and wondered if the women were talking as much as all these men.

≈

Inside the house, Sarah had put away the last of the dishes. Aunt Lilly and several of the other ladies complained of minor ailments that she would tend to quickly. Sarah made one more pot of tea—tea of chamomile. One by one, her guests seemed to get sleepy and excused themselves for bed. Sarah had placed sachets of hops and lilac on each pillow to help with sleep. Sarah smiled; thankful her mother had given her the knowledge about chamomile and sleep. Sarah settled down in Mack's room for the night. She turned the lamp out and smiled as the laughter of the men could be heard coming from the barn.

≈

Over the next two hours, Mack listened to Uncle Mike talk about the slaves he owned. He talked about how Frank Bowen never approved of owning slaves, so they were sent from his plantation to work the tobacco fields. Frank treated them kindly— plenty of water and food, no lash ever. The women were sent to help Elise. Frank did not allow them in the tobacco fields. Uncle Mike told them, "I have lost many of the young ones to the Underground Railroad. The fields were harder to work with the older men, but we manage."

James had been more upset over the taxation they had all faced. This conversation continued for most of the night. Mack closed her eyes and listened to James's voice as she tried to go to sleep. She could pick his voice out among all the others. His voice warmed and comforted her. This was a strange feeling, one she had never known until this night. Mack went to sleep with the warmth and love of friends.

The rooster crowing woke Mack. The morning sky showed no sun, just multiple shades of blue. She gathered her quilts, slipped silently toward the ladder, and attempted to leave without waking anyone. She paused to look at James. Did she hear Uncle Mike telling someone James would be twenty-two on his next birthday? As Mack ran from the barn to the house, she shivered from the chill of the morning air. Mack was sure the only thing to wake those left sleeping in the barn would be buckets of cold water.

Sarah stood in her blue-checkered day dress, looking out the back door. There was coffee brewing on the stove and fires burning in the fireplaces, warming the main rooms downstairs for visitors that would be down soon. She opened the door for Mack. "Hungry?" Sarah asked, trying not to laugh at the expression on Mack's face.

"I think that before I spend another night listening to men complain about women gaggling, I'll go back and sleep in that tree full of poison oak."

Sarah laughed.

"It isn't funny, Sarah. They talked all night, and Uncle Mike got drunk, snored, and then passed so much gas, I was worried the barn would burn down. Is the coffee done?"

"Mack, I have something for you. Maybe it will make up for Uncle Mike. I couldn't give it to you last night." Sarah reached in the warming cupboard, taking out a small package wrapped with bright paper and ribbon.

Mack smiled, her eyes wide, reaching. "For me?"

"Something I hope you'll enjoy over and over."

Mack tore frantically at the ribbon and wrappings. Tears ran down her cheeks.

"I has never got no gift like this before," Mack stammered, forgetting to use what Sarah had so patiently taught.

"Slow down, it will be fine." Sarah's heart was touched by Mack's reaction.

Mack hugged the little book and read the title aloud, "Jay.. .n Airee, by, by, Char.. .lotte Bron.. .Bron..t."

"We will read it together," Sarah said.

Sarah stood on the front steps and watched until the last wagon of family and friends were no longer in sight. It was late afternoon, and old Ben had been sent from the slave quarters to say she was needed. Sarah took Elise's medical pouch to the root cellar and gathered what she might need: salves, roots, garlic, oils, flowers and leaves for tea, and cotton and wool for poultices. When Sarah returned to the house, she found Mack in the main room asleep with the book on her chest. She covered her with a quilt, marked the page, and placed the book on the side table. Sarah made a final trip to the kitchen for food, tobacco, more coffee, blankets, and other items she had been gathering during the summer. There were children's clothes that families were going to throw out but which were still good. At the Methodist church on Sunday mornings, Sarah asked for any clothing to be saved for her.

Today she would take all that had been donated to the slave quarters. James had brought the wagon to the front of the house. Ben put the supplies in the back of the wagon. Sarah changed into a pair of Ethan's old pants and a shirt. She kept one of James's old coats and a pair of boots he could no longer wear.

"Sarah, I wish you would let me go with you," James all but begged.

"I will be fine," she reassured him. "Uncle Mike sent word he has two women ready to birth, and there are more children with fevers. Some of the older men have foot and hand injuries with green and white fluid draining from them. I appreciate your offer, but you are needed here. It could be a couple of days before I return. There is plenty of food for you and Mack."

James hugged his sister and sent her on her way. "Ben, if Miss Sarah needs anything, you send word."

"Yes, sir. I wills."

Sarah was the only help for Ben and the other slaves. Elise always told Sarah, "It matters not who the person is, it's what you can do to ease their suffering." As Sarah and Ben left, she knew this would be a long night for her.

James went back into the house and put more wood in the fireplace in the main room. He sat down across from Mack and thought about how fond he had become of this small boy who worked like a man but had such a gentle manner. This was a brave boy who planned to go off to war. He would be sad to see Mack leave. Sarah had grown attached to him, too. James got up and went out to check the animals and the last of the tobacco that was now dry and needed to be stacked. He was fortunate to have had a late crop. It would bring extra money. James knew that before long he would have to make a decision about joining the fight. He already felt guilty for not leaving when so many of the men in the county had already gone; many had died. He worried about Sarah and leaving her to run the farm.

He knew in his heart Sarah would never stay behind if he left. Hell, she might leave and he would have to join up to watch over her. She was a stubborn woman, who should have been married with a home of her own. The men that had attempted to call on Sarah were told in a firm manner that they should not come back unless they were sick. James had thought at times that Sarah might be waiting to meet Samuel, although she had never spoken of it. He didn't believe two people with different lifestyles could ever have anything in common. James shook his head and went to the barn to stack the last tobacco leaves. He knew it would be a few days before Sarah returned, enough time to make a fast trip to the warehouse and buy supplies in Augusta. James would tell Mack when he woke up. They would leave in the morning with the small wagon. The trip would do them both good. James walked back to the house and thought about his sister, hoping she would be okay.

~

Sarah arrived at the slave shacks. Rebecca and Agnes met her with greetings and urgent requests for all who needed treatment. Sarah assured them she would stay until everyone had been seen and the babies had come.

"I am not going anywhere until I am sure everyone is well," Sarah said.

Water boiled on several fires. Ben and some of the other men were unloading the wagon with the supplies she had brought to them.

"Miss Sarah, you do so much for us here," Rebecca said.

Sarah took her mother's pouch and removed the supplies she would need over the next few days. Rebecca and Agnes were given herbs and told to make teas.

Sarah then went to check the women in labor. Chloe was the first to be checked. She seemed to be in early labor with her first baby. The birthing pains were not close and Sarah worried that her water had broken many hours too soon.

"Rebecca, I want you to make Chloe a tea of wild black cherry. She needs to walk and not lay in the bed," Sarah instructed.

She showed Rebecca which bag contained the bark used for the tea.

Letty, the second woman in labor, was about to deliver her fifth child when Sarah arrived at the "Miss Sarah, yous almost missed this one," Letty said.

Sarah tried not to worry when she saw the butt of the baby instead of a head. She knew the chances of the baby's head getting caught was great. She washed her hands, took a towel, and as the butt and legs came, Sarah prepared for a problem, but with another push, the rest of the baby came with no incident.

She waited for the cord to stop pulsing, then tied and cut it. She silently thanked God above and wiped the sweat off her forehead on her sleeve. Rebecca and Agnes took the big boy to clean. Sarah waited for the afterbirth. The baby was returned and immediately placed on his mother's breast. Letty had no problem nursing this baby. When the afterbirth came, Sarah worried about heavy bleeding since Letty had such a big baby. She had Rebecca stay and watch for problems. Sarah showed Rebecca a place on Letty to rub and to call if it got soft or the bleeding became too much. Agnes cleaned Letty after the birth. They had helped Sarah with birthing over the last two years since her mother died. They could probably do this without her, but she was pleased they called her to come and see to their needs.

Sarah went to see the children.

There had been less illness and death due to Sarah's constant complaining to Uncle Mike. Soap was now made on a regular basis, and wood floors, instead of dirt, were built in most of the slave quarters. The children who had fevers were tended to with yarrow, meadowsweet herb, and black cherry juice. A tea of chamomile with a touch of honey was given for pain and to help them sleep. Sarah was thankful there had been no sign of pox or measles among the children.

The feet and hands of the older men were checked. The injuries they suffered from the fields could cause white or green fluids to form. They were cleaned with witch hazel and covered with a salve of marigolds and dandelions. Black salve drew the core of infections to the surface. Onion and garlic juice were used when Sarah felt salves were not needed.

The older women took black Cohosh to ease their suffering after their monthly cycles ended. She gave tobacco for complaints of toothaches. Comfrey would be used on broken bones. A garlic broth assisted with the healing process. Sarah made visits throughout the night with teas, juices, and broths. She gave thanks for no serious illnesses, nor anyone near death.

Chloe had not progressed. The young girl had been able to sleep some throughout the night. The morning turned into the second afternoon, and Sarah's concern increased for Chloe and her baby.

"Chloe, where are your pains?" Sarah asked.

"My back is paining me bad."

Sarah felt Chloe's belly to make sure the baby continued to move inside. She was relieved to feel the baby kick while checking the hardness of the pains.

"Rebecca, I need a large warm cloth," Sarah said."Chloe, I want you to come with me."

Sarah led Chloe to a large tree that had fallen over.

"I want you to face the tree, lean down on your arms, and move your hips side to side. I think your baby may be in a wrong position, and this may help."

Sarah rubbed oil of clary sage, lavender, and rose on the lower portion of Chloe's back and then placed the warm cloth that Rebecca had brought to her.

"Miss Sarah, go and lay down for a while. Betsy, Chloe's maw, and I will be taking care of her," Agnes said."We will comes get you when she gets closer. Yous have been up all night and needs to sleep. Rebecca and I took a time during the night to rest, but you ain't had none."

"I could use a little sleep. I think everyone else I have treated is doing well. Maybe I should go check the children first—," Sarah said, but she was cut off by Agnes.

"They's fine, Miss Sarah. Go sleep." Agnes now talked to Sarah like a mother.

"Okay, keep using the warm cloths for a while and have her rock, but wake me if there is a problem."

"Miss Sarah, go."

Sarah crawled up into the back of the wagon. She smiled when she saw hay. James was kind enough to put it there for her makeshift bed. Sarah lay down and covered herself with quilts. It was the last thing she remembered until Agnes woke her. Night had come to the quarters.

"Miss Sarah, can you comes? Chloe is pushing," Agnes told her. Agnes had brought some food, and Sarah ate while she walked to the shack where she could hear Chloe moaning and screaming. Sarah entered and saw Rebecca wipe sweat off Chloe's forehead. Rebecca helped her push.

"Come on, girl. You kin do this. Push that baby outta there," Rebecca softly told Chloe.

"How long has she been doing this?" Sarah asked Agnes.

"Not long. Just a bit after the sun went down."

Sarah placed her hands on Chloe's belly. The hardness was strong enough, but there was another problem. Chloe's skin had become hot; she now had a fever. Sarah feared she had a birthing illness that came when a baby took too long to be born. Sarah washed her hands and waited as signs appeared that were encouraging. Sarah could see the top of the baby's head as she used warm oil to keep the skin soft in hopes that there would not be a tear.

"Chloe," Sarah spoke softly. "Listen to me, and let your body do what it is made to do."

"Miss Sarah, help me," Chloe pleaded.

"I am, I promise. I will."

In three pushes, a tiny baby girl was born, screaming and wiggling.

"Thank you, Miss Sarah," Chloe said.

Sarah handed the baby to Betsy. The afterbirth came very fast and a lot of blood with it. Sarah called for the baby to be put to breast. The bleeding had not slowed as Sarah had hoped. The length of birthing caused an additional illness which did not help. Sarah called for her pouch. She found the bottle of chokecherry juice she brought to every delivery. Chloe was given the juice to drink, a bitter-tasting cure for heavy bleeding after birthing. The nursing of the baby and the juice helped. Sarah checked Chloe's belly, still hard. Sarah stayed at Chloe's bedside the rest of the night. Cool compresses were used on her hot skin until she could be safely given another herb.

"Betsy, I want you to go and get some broth with a small piece of bread for Chloe. Do any of you know if there is a wet nurse in the quarters?" Sarah asked.

The women talked among themselves for a few moments. "Sellah just finished nursing Lila's baby a few days ago," Betsy said.

"Can she nurse Chloe's baby for a few days? I want to make sure this illness doesn't continue. Rebecca, would you go see if Sellah is willing to help us?"

"Miss Sarah," Betsy started. "Mista Mike will want Chloe to go back to work."

"I will talk to Uncle Mike," Sarah said sternly.

∾

Sarah stayed in the slave quarters until the next morning. She rechecked the new mothers and babies. The bleeding had slowed to what it should be for both new mothers. Chloe had been resting, although her skin was still hot to the touch. Sarah gave her valerian-and-chamomile tea, and a hop-and-lavender sachet was placed close to her head to induce sleep. Sellah told Sarah the baby girl was having some trouble sucking but not to worry.

"I fed eleven a my own and have fed six others. I ain't gonna let this little bird get the best a me."

Sarah laughed and realized she couldn't keep her eyes open. The children treated for fevers were better, most running and playing now. She was amazed how quickly children recover. She rechecked hands and feet; they were retreated if necessary and redressed. The boils were lanced, cores removed, and then covered with healing creams to prevent further drainage.

Ben had been sent by Rebecca and Agnes to find Sarah. "Miss Sarah, you needs to go rest now," he begged.

"Yes, Ben. I think so," Sarah answered.

"God has blessed those of us here with you an' yours. Thank you for all you do and has done for us. We all miss Ms. Elise. It pained us all when she and Mista Frank passed," Ben said.

"Thank you, Ben. As long as we continue to speak of them, they are never truly gone."

"Yes'm, you is right, Miss Sarah. You is right."

"To heal makes my heart happy," Sarah said.

"You is our angel, Miss Sarah, yes, you is."

Ben helped Sarah into the wagon, and they start toward Uncle Mike's.

"Before I go home, I'll come back once more to check on everyone." Sarah mumbled.

When they arrived at the main house, Aunt Lilly and Uncle Mike helped Sarah out of the wagon.

"Sarah, are you hungry?" Aunt Lilly asked.

"No, just need to sleep." She stumbled to a bed and looked at Uncle Mike.

"When I wake up, we have to talk. There are things you need to fix," Sarah slurred her words.

Uncle Mike shook his head and said, "Tomorrow, girl. Tomorrow."

Sarah slept in her clothes until Aunt Lilly woke her the next morning.

"Sarah, Sarah." Lilly shook her gently.

"What? Is something wrong? Is everyone okay?" Sarah jumped out of bed.

"Stop, girl. Everyone is fine. James is outside with that boy, Mack. They have come to take you home."

Sarah rose to find Aunt Lilly had undressed her and cleaned the clothes she had been wearing.

Sarah found soap and fresh scented water to use before dressing. Once she had fixed her hair and wiped away the sleep from her eyes, Sarah went out to have breakfast. She was happy to see James and Mack sitting at the table eating.

Sarah sat down next to Mack."I could use a cup of tea. How many days has it been, Aunt Lilly?"

"You spent over two days and nights with the slaves, most of a day of sleeping. This morning makes four. You do too much," Lilly chastised.

Uncle Mike looked across the table.

"Uncle Mike, we have to talk about the shanty," Sarah started.

Uncle Mike looked at James for help.

"Don't look at me, Uncle Mike. You're the one with the slaves, and Sarah is the healer. You deal with her."

"Okay, girl. What needs to be done?" Uncle Mike grabbed a piece of paper and pencil.

"First the roofs need patching..." For the next few minutes, Sarah was the only one talking. "There are boards that the wind blows through; the floors need to be repaired. I didn't see enough soap, and when you go to town, you make sure they give you the good soap, not that cheap, harsh lye. They keep the good soap in the back, and you tell Mr. Jessup Sarah said to give you what I buy, or he will answer to me the next time I go to Augusta. I brought some blankets and clothes from the church, but they need more. The food supplies need to be increased with winter here. More wood for heat. Chloe is not to work for at least two weeks."

Sarah tried to remember if that was all that was needed.

James laughed so hard, tears ran down his face.

Mack's mouth was wide open. She remembered being told by her maw that you never disrespect your elders.

"Fine, fine. Okay, okay. I will take care of this," Uncle Mike groaned.

"That will be all the payment I need," Sarah told him. "My work goes for nothing if you do not help."

"I will, girl. I will," Uncle Mike promised.

"Sarah," James said. "Have you finished with Uncle Mike? We need to get back. Mack and I just dropped off the other wagon of supplies from Augusta. We still need to unload."

"You two went to Augusta together?" she asked.

"Yes," James answered. "Mack needed a trip off the farm, and I needed the extra help." James didn't understand Sarah's question or concern. "Mack is a lot of help, and the trip was good for both of us."

Mack got up and grabbed her cap. "I'm going to go check the horses," she said.

"Aunt Lilly, thank you for cleaning my clothes," Sarah said.

"Girl, you were so funny when I took them off you. You kept mumbling about Mack's lessons, doing laundry, drying more herbs," Lilly laughed.

They all walk outside where the wagon had been brought for their trip home. James helped Sarah into the wagon.

"James, we have to stop at the shanties on the way home. I have to check everyone," she said.

"I figured as much. I had Mack go to the cellar and get what she was familiar with for you."

Mack tied James's horse behind the wagon and swung up in her saddle and followed them to the shanties.

When Sarah arrived to check on everyone in the quarters, Rebecca, Agnes, and Betsy walked with her.

There were a few cuts to be tended with another change of bandages. Chloe and her baby were fine, fever gone, and Sarah's relief was apparent to everyone. She talked with Chloe and explained that it might be a few days before she had milk but to keep nursing the baby, and then let Sellah have her.

"Betsy, do you know where there is blessed thistle or milk thistle?" Sarah asked.

Rebecca responded, "Miss Sarah, I has sum saved. Your maw taught me about the thistle years ago."

"Good. Chloe should take a tea of it once a day until her milk increases," Sarah explained. "Betsy, I want Chloe to eat

the garlic broth once a day for a week. If you have questions, Rebecca or Agnes can tell you how much to use." Sarah took the rest of the garlic from the wagon and gave it to Betsy.

"Rebecca, if Chloe becomes ill in the next few days, send Ben quickly for me. The fever could return."

"Yes'm, I will," Rebecca answered.

"Thank you, Miss Sarah," Betsy said, smiling and holding her grandbaby.

"I spoke with Uncle Mike, and there will be no work for Chloe for two weeks," Sarah told them, smiling.

All three women look surprised.

"And he will be here with supplies for repairs. That is my charge. I will be back to check and make sure he is good on his word," Sarah finished.

All three laughed, and Agnes said, "Miss Sarah, you has a heavy hand, but fairs."

Sarah looked at the tiny baby Betsy held. "Does she have a name yet?" Sarah asked.

"Yes, ma'am," Chloe started. "If it's okay with yous. I would like to be calling her Sarah Ann."

"I am honored."

Sarah encouraged Mack to follow her throughout the shanties to observe and learn how nature was used when doctors were not available.

"Mack, you brought the right herbs. You seem to be learning quickly about everything. You will have to tell me about your trip to Augusta," Sarah teased.

Mack's face turned red, and she headed back toward the wagon.

Agnes and Rebecca were given all of the herbs that Sarah had left. There was a lot of work to do to make living and working better.

Sarah climbed into the wagon where Mack had already tied her horse and jumped into the back. James slapped the horses with the reins, and they headed for home.

Sarah heard laughter and turned to see the children whom she had treated running after the wagon as it left, smiling and waving at her.

Chapter 6

THE WHITE MANSION
VALENTINE'S DAY SATURDAY
FEBRUARY 14, 1863

Julia lay laboring on the bed, as Eric wiped her forehead again.
She had been in pain for hours. The pains had started the day
before, mild at first. Julia had been able to ignore them and
even sleep. Then they became closer together, so she began to
walk, use the rocking chair, and move until her water broke.
The downstairs guest room, where she had spent so many
days, would now be where their child was born, hers and
Eric's. Lucy, Julia's most trusted member of the house staff
and a friend, had been gathering old linens for weeks, washing
and folding them to prepare for this day. A fire kept the room
warm, although Julia did not need it. She did not feel cold. The
lamps were turned low.

"Eric, help me. Another one is coming," Julia told him.

He helped support her as she started to push. Although this
seemed unusual, Eric had done this in the past with his beloved
Eleanor. As a man of power and wealth, he knew there were
nurses and house staff who could take his place. Yet, he felt
humbled by the miracle of birth and felt a need to be here. The
thought of losing another woman he loved was more than he
could bear. He would remain and support his wife.

"Daniel, Julia has been pushing for a long time," Eric said, his voice was filled with concern for his wife.

Dr. Develle laughed, "Eric, you need a new pocket watch. It has truly been only one hour since she started to push. Julia, you're almost finished. One more push."

And with that last push, a small figure emerged.

Phillip Alfred White was born at 4:00 a.m., without difficulty or fanfare, to Julia and Eric. He seemed a little small, but he made his presence known loudly. Dr. Develle gave his full approval to the newest member of the family and handed Phillip to Eric, who quickly dried and wrapped his son in a new blanket. Lucy then cleaned Julia up and helped her into a dry gown. Clean linens were replaced on the bed beneath her. Eric was patient while this took place; so many men had no idea what happens during childbirth or why it takes so long, and most never would. He looked at the tiny being in his arms. Tiny hands reached and grabbed his finger.

"My God, I had forgotten," he said out loud.

"Eric, can I hold our son?" Julia asked.

He sat down on the bed with his beautiful wife and handed Phillip to her. She wiped the tears from her face.

"He's perfect," she said.

Julia put Phillip to her breast, and he quickly decided that eating was better than crying. Julia had not wasted time the last weeks of her pregnancy in ignorance. She had talked with other mothers and took advice on birthing, nursing, and healing. She wanted to be a good mother, and all the questions she asked had paid off. Her baby was nursing, the bleeding was not heavy, and she was thankful for the miracle that now suckled at her breast. She would not have maids and nannies take care of Phillip; she would.

Dr. Develle gathered his belongings and headed toward the bedroom door.

Eric shook his hand.

"Daniel, thank you."

"Oh, don't worry. My bill will be here soon enough," Daniel laughed. "I'll be back later in the day to check on Julia and the baby."

Daniel Develle turned, and with as stern a look as possible toward his patient said, "Julia, I would like for you to stay in bed and rest, but I feel my words are falling on deaf ears. Have Lucy send for me if you should have problems."

Julia smiled. "I will."

Eric knew that she would rest for now, but later she would be up. Lucy promised to help her so she would heal more quickly. Most women laid in bed for days. His wife was too independent and couldn't stand the thought of doing that, letting others clean her. She would take care of herself—with Lucy's help.

The morning sky had become lighter, and the staff prepared breakfast. Eric had decided to stay home today. The work at the dock could be handled by the people he put in charge. Good people that had been mistreated by Atwood. Eric took the fancy office and turned it into a place for the men to go when the weather was disagreeable. The extra items inside were given to charity after Louisa took what she wanted. The bank closed on Saturday and Sunday. Today would be for family. Eric looked up as Emily and Ellen tiptoed in to see Phillip.

They laughed and were allowed to hold their brother. They were old enough to help Julia with the baby and had been excited and anxious these past few weeks. Eric kissed his wife.

"Girls, your mother needs to rest." Eric was gentle in his request.

Both girls kissed Julia and ran off for breakfast. Lucy took the baby so that Julia could rest. As Lucy bent down to take Phillip, Julia whispered, "No later than noon, Lucy."

"Yes, ma'am. I will."

"Mr. White, Mr. Franklin is in the library waiting for you. I had coffee and pastries taken in for both of you."

"Thank you, Lucy."

Eric worried this might not be good news.

Eric had talked with Franklin late last evening when Julia's pains were beginning.

There was nothing of importance at that time. Eric quickened his steps on the way to the library. He tried to relax the furrow that increased between his eyes: a trait he had developed since obtaining Atwood's assets. When Eric opened the doors, he was relieved to see Franklin sitting by the fire drinking coffee and eating.

"Good morning and congratulations, old friend," Franklin stood. "Eric, you look terrible."

They shook hands and hugged one another. Franklin handed Eric a box of cigars.

"From my private collection. I am having flowers delivered later for Julia," he said, smiling.

"And where did you find fresh flowers?"

"I have my connections, and being friends with one of the wealthiest men in New York helps." Franklin grinned. "Tomorrow there will be a special edition announcing the birth of—? Eric, is it a boy or a girl?"

"It is a boy."

"And does this young man have a name yet?"

"Julia refused to pick a girl's name. She was so certain it would be a boy. We have kept the name a secret from everyone, and it's my honor, old friend, to tell you after all you have done for this family over the years. Our son's name will be Phillip, after Julia's father, and Alfred, after our closest and dearest friend."

Franklin remained silent and then cleared his voice to speak, but no words formed at that moment. He turned and wiped the tears from his face. Franklin saw the last week's Weekly lying on Eric's desk opened to Samuel's recent story about the war.

"He is making quite a name for himself," Franklin finally found a voice to speak.

"I know, and I am proud of him," Eric said. "These stories are not easy to read. I cannot imagine how hard they were to write when you experience them firsthand."

"Have you been reading the featured article he is writing?"

"The one called 'The Women Who Travel in War'?"

"Yes. I have been notified by numerous papers and other weekly magazines. They are asking permission to run these articles in their papers. There are monetary offers. That was the other reason I am here. Samuel and I need to have your solicitors draw up a contract. These articles could make Samuel a lot of money, and I have been contacted by a publisher about gathering all the stories once they are finished and placing them in book form."

Eric was shocked, happy, and relieved all once.

"It will be my pleasure, my friend."

"Wonderful," Franklin told him. "Now I will leave you to your beautiful wife and new son."

He picked up his wool overcoat and started for the library doors.

"Franklin, thank you."

Franklin smiled and said nothing as he left the library.

Eric listened for the last of Franklin's footsteps, and then returned to his desk to look through the entire Weekly for Samuel's first article that seemed to be causing so much interest. He hated to lie to his old friend, but the main stories were enough for him to read.

He found the article in question. Samuel introduced the readers to the horrific scene at Fredericksburg in the operating theatre. He told how the women never faltered to do their jobs in the worst of conditions. Samuel watched these women hold the hands of dying men, their dresses stained with blood after cleaning and bandaging wounds. They comforted boys crying for their mothers. Samuel then talked about Florence Nightingale and Clara Barton. He praised them and their work.

Eric continued to read and couldn't understand why any woman would subject herself to the dangers of war. Would Julia follow me to war, be at my side, and possibly die? Ridiculous! He doubted these articles would go as far as Franklin thought. He would be good on his word and contact the solicitors on Monday. Who would possibly be interested in women that would subject themselves to the horrors of war? Eric put the Weekly back down on the desk and went to the dining room to join his daughters for breakfast. His thoughts were no longer on the war or the women who put themselves in harm's way.

Chapter 7

Mack had finished packing. She tried to take only what would be needed, as she must be able to travel light and fast. Mack ran her hand over the book Sarah gave her for Christmas. The page where she stopped reading was bent. Mack had now read Jane Eyre twice. She quickly put the book in the inside pocket of her coat. This was the day she had been working toward. She felt excitement, and also sadness. Mack looked at the valentine she had made for James.

She had written a letter detailing her deception and the reasons for it and then asking for his forgiveness. She had made Sarah promise to give it to him after she left. Mack couldn't face him knowing she had lied all these months. It would be even harder now that she had grown to have feelings for him.

"Mack, breakfast.," Sarah called. "Don't forget your book."

Mack thought Sarah's tone was sad when she called. Everything she owned was packed and brought downstairs.

"Where's James?" Mack asked.

"He is gone to Augusta. He left before I was up." Sarah answered.

"I guess it makes things a little easier knowing I don't have to face him."

Mack's feelings were hurt, but she knew this was for the best. She needed to go while he was gone. She might actually cry, and that would not be manly.

"Do you know where you're headed?" Sarah asked.

Mack could hear the tears caught in her throat.

"Toward Fort McAllister. I'll start there and see where the road leads me."

The two women ate breakfast together, discussing all they had learned from each other.

"You have been a good student. Just remember not to get in a hurry, and you will do fine," Sarah said."Mack, James knew you were going to leave one day and wanted you to take one of the horses. You'll make better time. I think he is worried about you, even though you are a fellow." They both laughed.

"I can't do that, Sarah. I have no money to give to you or James. It wouldn't be right."

"Let's just call it a loan. You can bring him back one day. I know you will be back this way again."

Mack was surprised and happy she would not have to walk. She had a sense of honor and knew it was not right to take what she could not pay for, but a loan might be okay.

"Yes, I will," Mack promised. Mack walked outside to see her mount—Grey Morning. Grey belonged to James. He had been saddled and ready to go. Mack had a special feeling with Grey. The horse could almost read her mind at times.

"Sarah, this is James's horse," Mack said.

"Well, he was until you came. It seems this horse prefers you to James."

Sarah had already packed food, another set of warm boy's clothes, monthly cycle items, an extra blanket, a pouch of herbs with instructions, and a list of medicinal herbs for her to look for along the way.

"Mack, I packed extra coffee and tobacco. It might help you to barter and keep yourself out of trouble."

"I can't find words for what you and James have done for me. You have been so patient. I am not the person I was two months ago. I am blessed to have you and James as my friends," Mack said as tears began to fall.

"I do not have words for what you did for Ethan. You have been a good pupil—smart and quick. Remember what you have learned, and listen to all that is around you."

"I will."

The two hugged each other. Sarah watched as Mack swung her small body into the saddle. She took her cap and put it on. Grey Morning was waiting for Mack to start their journey.

"I will come back," Mack said.

Sarah nodded her head.

"Tell James.. .I.. .I—" Mack couldn't finish.

"It'll be fine. I will tell him."

Mack turned her mount and headed toward the gate she had entered two months ago. She would not look back because Mack knew if she did she would never leave. She was a different person now—happy, wiser, and ready for another adventure. She pretended to check her knife and wiped the tears away on her sleeve.

⌒

Sarah stood at the front door and watched until she could no longer see Mack. As Sarah walked back inside, she silently prayed. Lord in heaven, watch over that young twig...

February 16, 1863

Midmorning on Monday, James had returned from Augusta with supplies.

Sarah met him in the kitchen with Mack's letter. She held the valentine back, waiting to see his reaction.

"Mack's gone, isn't he?" "Yes."

Within a few minutes of reading the letter, James's face turned red. He tried holding back the words that were forming, but he exploded.

"You knew? The entire time she was here, you knew and said nothing? Does anyone else know? Does any of the family know? Am I the only fool here?"

"James, please listen to me. It was Mack's decision not to tell you or anyone else. She made me promise."

James paced the kitchen floor, stomping.

"I don't understand why she couldn't tell me," he said, his tone lowered.

"Why don't you read the rest of the letter. It might explain and answer all your questions." Sarah was begging.

"Have you read this?"

"No!" Sarah tried not to shout."Why would I? She wrote it to you. James, try and understand Mack's reasons for not telling you."

"I don't know if I can."

James walked out, slamming the kitchen door. He grabbed the reins of the team and took them and the wagon toward the barn to unload supplies.

Sarah shook her head. She had known this was not going to go well when Mack left, but it had to be done. Sarah started out the back door in an attempt to reason with James, but the sound of a wagon and horses stopped her.

∽

Ruby Belle, a large woman of forty pulled her wagon and team of horses onto the Bowen farm. She wore a large, tan, wide-brimmed hat tied down with a brown ribbon, and a few strands of reddish brown hair hung out beneath it. She kicked the brake in place and took off the leather gloves she wore to handle the reins.

Five younger women crawled out of the back of the wagon, and two women who were dressed the same ran to help Ruby Belle down.

Sarah walked out to greet these unexpected visitors. Leaving James alone would be the best thing to do right now. She took Mack's valentine and put it in her apron pocket.

Ruby Belle shook the dust off her brown day dress and looked up to see a young woman walking toward her in a blue-checkered day wrapper and apron, blonde hair pulled into a bun.

"Young miss, is your mother here?" Ruby Belle began."We have been told there is a healer here about, and I have a need to speak with her. I am Ruby Belle from New Orleans, and we are southern nurses in need of supplies, food, and a place to rest. If your mother is not the healer we have heard about for the last two days, is it possible for you to give us directions to her home?"

Sarah was surprised. These women were looking for her.

"Ms. Belle, I am Sarah Bowen. I am the healer you are seeking.

Ruby Belle hugged Sarah, almost picking her up off her feet and said, "Thank God above. Girls, we found her. You seem a might young to be the healer we have been hearing about."

I think I can explain it better if all of you would come inside, please, where it is warmer. Let me fix something for you to eat."

"We thank you kindly, Miss Sarah, but we will not be a burden. We will help, won't we, girls?" Ruby turned and waited for the proper reply. She was not disappointed when all answered in the affirmative.

"Miss Sarah, we have been on the road many days. Most of us need a wash for ourselves and clothes," Sallie, one of the twins, told Sarah.

"Ruby Belle, it will be my pleasure to offer you and your ladies the comforts you require," Sarah smiled.

"God bless you, girl," Ruby shouted.

As Sarah opened the back door, Ruby Belle, made her way inside.

"The two coming in behind me are my daughters," Ruby told Sarah.

Sadie introduced herself and pointed to a scar on her right arm that Sallie didn't have.

"Miss Sarah, now you can tell the difference between me and Sallie."

Sarah was glad to have some reference to tell them apart, as they were mirror images of each other with the same reddish hair as their mother.

Ruby Belle went into the kitchen and made herself at home, pulling pans out of cupboards and giving the other women orders to help Sarah with washtubs and pumping water.

Sarah was amazed at how well these women all worked together and followed Ruby's instructions without argument. In just an hour, food had been prepared, clothes were being soaked, and Sarah had set the table for seven. Sarah tried to hide how anxious she was to ask questions about the war and how she could be of help to these women. It was obvious to Sarah that even though proper manners were being enforced by Ruby Belle, it had been some time since these women had a proper meal.

Sarah made sure that each woman's plate remained filled, and no one left the table until they were full. She looked across the table at a frail, young woman picking at her food. Sarah had seen the small bulge when she came into the house with the others.

"How far along are you, miss?" Sarah inquired.

"Emma, Miss Sarah. My name is Emma, and I am six months along. I am going to meet my betrothed, Leonard, so we can be a family." Emma smiled and patted her small belly.

Sarah handed Emma an extra piece of meat and encouraged her to eat. She was concerned at the small size of Emma's belly. At six months along, Sarah felt the young woman should be bigger.

When the meal was finished, Ruby Belle had the younger girls clear the table. All of the women came back and sat waiting for Ruby to begin.

"Miss Sarah, we need anyone and everyone that can help in the war to take care of our men who are fighting. There is much we do not know, and we need a healer. Someone who is willing to teach us and maybe help stop so many of our men from dying from the injuries of war, illnesses, and the flux we can't stop."

"What about the doctors and their medicine?" Sarah asked.

"The war is so wide and vast that supplies are few. Many times we have had to stand by and watch young men die a horrible death. We have been told by the good folks of this area that you heal with nature. Is this true?"

"Yes." Sarah got up at that moment and went to get her mother's pouch. Sarah took out the books that had been her guide and laid them on the table for the others to see. "My mother was the healer in this county for many years while my father farmed. I grew up in this house learning how to heal with nature."

Leona, the youngest of the group, looked through the books and listened closely to Sarah but said nothing.

"Most of us sitting at this table have some knowledge, but it is very limited, and we cannot recognize the plants needed to heal or the proper usage," Ruby explained.

"For God's peace, Ruby, just ask the woman, please," Maud finally spoke. "Sarah, honey, you have to excuse me. I am a Texas woman, and we just don't take this long to ask questions. Hell, look at me out here hunting for the man I married a year ago."

"I'm getting there, Maud," Ruby said. "Sarah, will you come with us, teach us, and help us take care of our boys in war?"

"I am not sure the doctors will approve of my healing practices," Sarah responded.

"Hell, woman. What they don't know won't hurt, and it might just help keep someone from dying," Maud firmly said.

Sarah didn't know what to say. She knew that she needed to do this. She wanted to go, and must go.

The time she had known would come had arrived.

"Ladies, if you could give me a few days, I will give you an answer by the end of the week. I need to speak with my brother and family before I make such a major decision."

"Fair enough. If you will let us stay here, I promise my girls will clean, cook, and do chores to pay for your hospitality," Ruby Belle stated proudly."We need to find medical supplies and make bandages. We have used all we had in our journey."

"I can help with that, too. The church saves old clothes, blankets, and linens for me. Our church has a special prayer service on Wednesday evenings since the war has started. We can collect any items that have been saved for me. Will you ladies join me?" Sarah asked.

"We'd be honored. It's been awhile since we had a chance to go to services," Ruby told Sarah.

∽

James had put away all the supplies, unhitched the horses, brushed, and fed them. He had tried to stay away from the house as long as possible until he was no longer angry at Sarah. He had just carried the coffee and flour out of the barn when he saw the wagon. He didn't recognize the horses as being from Uncle Mike's or Uncle Earl's.

"Now what?" James said out loud. He wondered who Sarah had invited into the house. He intended to tell whoever it was they couldn't stay. James opened the back door and went to the pantry to put away the flour and coffee, when he heard voices in the main room. He slowly walked toward the voices—women's voices.

Sarah had heard the back door open. She stood and turned around in time to see James frozen in place, looking at the six women sitting at the main table. The look on James's face was unforgettable. Sarah would never know if it was shock or horror. He would never admit to either.

He turned and went out the back door. Sarah followed him.

"James, please wait. Let me explain," Sarah started.

"I can't do this right now, Sarah. I have had all the surprises I can take for one day," James told her, his voice beginning to show strain.

James quickened his pace toward the barn. Sarah continued to follow him.

"Where are you going?"Sarah asked.

"To Uncle Mike's or Uncle Earl's, I am not sure. I just know I can't stay here," James walked into the barn and reached for his saddle.

"How long will you be gone?"

"I don't know."

Sarah stood and watched him saddle and mount his horse. She wanted to talk to him, to make him understand about Mack, and explain about the women in the house. She felt nothing she could say would change anything at this point. As he started to leave, Sarah reached in her apron pocket and handed him the valentine Mack had made for him.

James took the red heart and put it in his pocket without reading it. He never spoke.

Sarah watched her brother ride out the gate.

It would be over two years before she saw him again.

Leona was standing at the back door when Sarah turned around. She walked out the door and quietly moved next to Sarah.

"Miss Sarah, are you all right?" Leona asked.

Sarah took a deep breath. "Yes, I will be fine. Leona, isn't it?"

"Yes, ma'am."

"I saw you looking at my mother's books. Would you like to see where I keep my herbs?" Sarah inquired.

"That would be nice."

Sarah and Leona went back inside where the laughter of women helped to ease the pain of James leaving without saying good-bye.

Friday morning, at dawn, Sarah visited the graves of James and Elise Bowen to say good-bye for now. She held the heart necklace tight, asking silently, Mother, help me, guide me so that I will be able to heal, teach, and give comfort as you taught.

"Sarah, daylight's a burning, girl. We need to go," Ruby Belle bellowed.

Sarah turned and walked to the wagon where hands reached out to help her into the back. She looked at each of these women she had known for only a few days. They were going to travel across the land to help those who suffered, to give peace to the dying, and for one of them to find the man she loved. She wrapped her mother's shawl around her shoulders and looked at the supplies taken from her home in preparation for the unknown. The church was generous, and many of the parishioners made an extra trip to bring extra items that could be used for bandages.

Sarah watched her home grow smaller as the wagon moved farther down the road. She thought of her friend Samuel. What would he think of her making this independent decision? Sarah's only regret was not finding James and talking out their differences. She hoped he would understand when he read the letter she left him. It was her turn to make a difference in the war; it was her turn to leave.

Chapter 8

James,

People are not always what they seem. I guess I am one of those.

You have known me as Mack Keens, a fourteen-year-old boy, hard worker, and I hope a friend. My true name is Martha Ann Catherine Keens. I am eighteen and truly sorry about the lie Sarah and I have told you these past months.

A promise made is a promise kept, and Sarah was good on her word to me. The time has come for me to keep the promise I made to my maw. I must go and help our boys in gray.

I have tried to find words for the feelings I have for you but cannot. So, I left you my heart.

I hope in time you will forgive me.

Mack

Mike stood drinking coffee, watching his nephew from the kitchen door. When James had shown up asking for a room, he had not questioned him. When James passed out from too much home brew, he'd covered him with a blanket. Now he watched James bring his mount out and start to saddle up.

"You had better go talk to him, Michael," Lilly said.

"I don't think anything I can say to him will change what he has planned."

"It doesn't matter. Go anyway. He's your kin."

Mike walked out the back door and toward James who was cinching up his saddle. He hoped to get some indication as to what James had planned and the reason.

"You want to talk about this?" Mike asked.

"Nope," James responded.

"You heading back home?"

"Nope. I have something I need to do."

"Does Sarah know you're not coming back?" Mike dug further.

"Nope."

"Dammit, James! What in blazes am I supposed to tell her?"

"Tell her it's personal," James said in a mild voice, never looking at his uncle.

Mike became frustrated and knew that any more questions would only be met with no defined answer.

James turned and shook his uncle's hand, then got on his horse. He had turned his mount to leave when he saw Aunt Lilly coming with supplies.

"Take care of yourself and come back home safe, you hear?" Lilly told him.

Mike could hear her holding back her tears.

"Thank you, Aunt Lilly. I will do what I can to stay in one piece." James finally smiled.

Mike and Lilly watched James leave.

"I can't understand those boys—first Ethan sneaking off in the dead of night and now James leaving for no real reason," Mike told his wife, shaking his head in disbelief, as he turned and walked away.

"Where are you going?" Lilly asked.

"I'm getting the horses and the wagon. Go get your bonnet, woman. We're taking a ride."

"Why?"

"You don't honestly think I am going to go face Sarah Jane alone, do you?" Mike shouted back at his wife.

~

It had been a grim trip to his brother's farm, unsure what either he or Lilly was going to say to Sarah. Both hoped that she would be able to shed some light on James and his sudden decision to ride off with no clear destination.

"Michael, there is no smoke coming from the chimney, and Sarah should have heard us coming through the gate," Lilly told her husband.

"Sarah may be out in the barn or that damned root cellar." Mike tried to stay his wife's fears.

"Michael, something is wrong here. What in God's name is going on in this house?" Lilly was almost in tears.

"I'm not sure."

Mike pulled up to the front door and helped Lilly down. She ran to the door and knocked. No answer. Mike walked up behind her and opened the door. The house was quiet, empty, a feeling it had been abandoned—no fires, no smell of food cooking or coffee brewing.

"Sarah? Sarah Jane? Where are you, girl?" Mike bellowed.

"Michael, maybe you're right and she's in the cellar. I'll go check."

Mike walked through the house and upstairs, looking in bedrooms. Beds were made, no sign of theft or damage.

Lilly entered the kitchen and saw the letter to James lying on the small breakfast table. She knew the proper thing to do would be to keep it until James returned, but she knew James would not be coming home and was now concerned about Sarah. Lilly opened the letter and read it. She then realized that James did not know Sarah had left.

"Michael!" Lilly screamed.

Mike ran downstairs, almost falling, thinking the worst. "What woman? Are you okay? Did you find Sarah?"

"Michael! Sarah has gone off with some women that were here last week. She said she is going to go be a nurse." Lilly trembled. She handed Mike the letter.

"What women? James didn't say there were any women in the house."

Lilly sat down and looked up at her husband. "What are we going to do?" She began to cry.

Mike looked up from the letter and walked to the back door. A moment later, he turned and faced his wife.

"We are going to gather the family, everyone who is close. We have to keep the farm up until someone comes back or—" Mike stopped, not wanting to worry his wife.

"Or what, Michael?" she asked.

"Lil, I don't want to think about the other right now." He put his arm around Lilly's shoulder as they secured the house, then got in their wagon, and went back to make plans to save his brother's legacy.

∽

Several hours after Mike and Lilly left to make a plan to save Bowen land, a stranger arrived seeking Sarah Bowen. He had an important letter to delivery all the way from Virginia. When he could get no answer to his knock, he left the letter under a rock on the front porch and proceeded on to his other deliveries. What this young man did not see was the raccoon that quickly moved the rock and ran off into the trees with the letter from Samuel.

Chapter 9

Samuel, for the love of God, will you please go home? It's Sunday, and I am sick of looking at you," Franklin said, laughing as he pulled out his bottle of bourbon and two glasses. "Haven't you done enough work since November?" he asked, as he filled the two glasses and pushed one toward Samuel.

"Let me finish putting these reports back," Samuel pleaded. He looked at his first report on Fredericksburg, then the second battle known as "the Mud March." He followed up with the replacement of General Ambrose Burnside with General Joseph Hooker after those disasters. Samuel's stories of the battles at Fort McAllister continued with more Union losses.

His special articles on "The Women Who Travel in War" continued to progress as he had hoped. The contract his father's solicitors and Franklin arranged had built a nice bank account—money that Samuel had a plan to use for a special project once the war had ended.

"Franklin, did I tell you I have been gathering interviews with nurses on the battlefields? I think it's time they tell their stories."

"Don't you think you are being a little hard on the Sanitation Commission? The last article on your special hit pretty low."

"If those men would spend less time arguing and spend more time listening and talking to Dorothea Dix and Clara Barton, more men might survive instead of dying from battle injuries, typhus, and flux." Samuel was stern but decided to try and lighten the conversation. "Have you heard the stories about women actually fighting on the battlefield next to men?"

"I simply cannot believe any of those stories. How could a woman disguise herself as a man? Has anyone seen a woman dressed as a soldier? Has anyone found a woman on the battlefield? Impossible."

"Let me tell you the rumor that was being told around the Army of the Potomac during the Fredericksburg campaigns. I cannot prove or disprove the story that was told to me by several soldiers. A recently promoted sergeant, who had served his duties well during the battles, gave birth to a rather large baby boy in January of this year. I searched for this woman or anyone who could substantiate the rumors during the rest of my assignment in Fredericksburg. What a story that would have been if I could have found that soldier."

"She didn't exist," Franklin firmly said.

"Who do I thank for paying my commutation fee? You or my father?" Samuel asked.

"Your father couldn't pay the money fast enough for you and George."

"It is sad to know the wealthy can buy their way out of fighting in the war."

"Have you started your story on the Gray Ghost?" Franklin asked, changing the subject.

"It's finished and ready for print," Samuel replied smartly.

"Samuel, I received a report from Clarence Smith about another Confederate spy that is easing in and out of Union camps like smoke. He managed to steal vital information about future battle plans from one Union camp, food, medical supplies, and he stole—" Franklin was laughing so hard tears were forming. "This spy stole eight cavalry horses and their leather under the noses of numerous camp guards. The soldiers had to walk to the closest camp for more mounts. No one can find him—no one can even give a description of him. The Union soldiers have named him the Night Walker."

"The Night Walker. Good name for him. Sounds like a story in the making, doesn't it?" Samuel smiled and finished his second bourbon.

"When are you leaving?" Franklin asked.

"I am leaving tomorrow afternoon. Julia has a special luncheon planned. She said that I have lost too much weight since I left New York. She has food stuffed into my mouth every chance she gets. You will be there, right?"

"Absolutely, I would never miss a family gathering. I need to check on young Phillip. I am sure he needs his special uncle to come and see him," Franklin said grinning."It's hard to believe you have been home only a week."

"Well, you see, I work for this very driven boss who demands the best from his reporters," Samuel joked.

"You can take all the time you want between assignments, you know that? It has been nice to have you back in the office," Franklin told him. "I believe it's you who is driven and pushing too hard."

"Maybe next time, boss. I want plenty of time to get to Washington, North Carolina. I really hadn't planned to come home. I missed the battle at Fort Anderson and do not plan to miss this one. Hopefully, I can run into this Night Walker and get the real story on his involvement in the war."

"I feel another 'Samuel White Special' in the works." Franklin followed Samuel to the door. "Good night. See you tomorrow."

"Good night, boss." Samuel grabbed his jacket and headed up the hill to the place he called home.

Samuel had forgotten to ask Julia if there were any letters from his friend. She should have sent one by now. Samuel had so much to tell her about his new assignment, and he was anxious to hear if the war had come to Waynesboro.

Chapter 10

TENNESSEE/NORTH CAROLINA BORDER

Mack Keens sat down with four Union soldiers to share the jug she offered as a friendly gesture so she could get food and information, and draw close to the fire. These renegades had given her no names, but it was easy to keep them separated. There was one tall and slim one who said he had left his home before the law caught up with him. He never mentioned the reason but seemed to enjoy killing the rabbit he had snared with his hands. The one with the full beard, who demanded the respect of the others, seemed to be the oldest of the group. No one questioned him. The other two boys were probably not much older than Mack; one was so fat his Union uniform barely fit, and the other had a face full of pockmarks. These four were more than willing to swap stories; most of the ones she would tell were lies. The soldiers had been talking about the battle at Fort Donaldson and the Union victory. They were on their way to Washington, North Carolina, just to see if they could help out. These men had no allegiance to any one group. They went, fought, then took what they wanted, and disappeared. These bastards fought for the enjoyment of killing and taking what was not theirs.

"Where'd you get the tobacco and coffee? I ain't seen none in a while." Mack talked slowly and hoped her drawl wasn't too bad.

"Boy, we took it off a wagon full of women who said they were nurses," the fat one told Mack.

"Prostitutes more like it,". the pockmarked one said.

"Yeah, there were two that looked and talked the same. A skinny pregnant girl and a young cute girl that didn't talk much. I kind of liked the way she smiled at me," the oldest of the group told Mack.

Mack didn't like him. He made her skin crawl, so she kept her knife close enough to use if necessary.

"My choice was that blonde, the blue-eyed one that called herself Sarah," the tallest one of the group told Mack."I bet she would be fine if I could have gotten her alone. I was about to take that one when a tfat woman and one they called Maud came out of the trees holding guns. We never saw them until it was too late. Maud told me she'd gut me and hang me over a tree to rot if we didn't get on down the road. We took their tobacco and coffee, got on our horses, and left."

Could Sarah have really left the farm? Mack decided at this point that she needed to get as much information from these fools as possible.

"Did them prostitutes tell you where they was going?" Mack asked.

"Same place we is headed: Washington, North Carolina," the pockmarked boy said, smiling at Mack.

"You need to join up with us," the oldest said.

Mack knew this man was not asking but rather demanding she join up with this group. "I ain't got a horse. I don't intend to walk to the battle." Mack sent the jug around again.

"Hell, boy you can ride with me. I got room," the fat one laughed.

"We might run into them nurses again and could use one more to help us get what we need this time," the tall one said, grinning.

"Be glad to join you," Mack told them.

They drank the two jugs Mack had stolen from a local moonshiner quickly. She had learned to cover the opening with her thumb when she raised the jug to keep from drinking—a good trick to get information and keep her wits.

When this group of bastards passed out and the fire died, Mack did what she did best. She disappeared into the darkness unheard and unnoticed by the rest. Mack changed clothes and stowed them for the next time a Union uniform was needed. She called for Grey, who came silently. The only thing on Mack's mind was finding Sarah to warn her, help her. She had to meet her contact with Longstreet's forces in two days. She had information about Chancellorsville that must be passed onto J. E. B. Stuart. Mack would then go to Washington and see if she could find Sarah.

Chapter 11

MARCH 16, 1863
SOUTH OF GREENVILLE, NORTH CAROLINA

Ruby Belle and her girls had settled into an abandoned farmhouse they found a few days earlier just south of Greenville, North Carolina.

Sarah was grateful they had found a place of safety after the incident with the Union soldiers. A chill ran down her back thinking of the way those men looked at her and the rest of the women.   Sarah knew that the coffee and tobacco they offered were not what those men wanted. Ruby Belle and Maud had saved all of them. She felt safe now.

Sarah had found an uncontaminated creek and pond that were close to the house. Contaminated water was something they ran across numerous times after leaving Waynesboro. When clean water was found, they collected all that they could find.

Sarah smiled thinking of the way Ruby Belle made friends with several moonshiners on the way to North Carolina. Ruby flirted and cooked some meals in exchange for a supply of medicinal alcohol and some barrels needed for water.

Since there were so many issues with clean water, Sarah insisted that all the water be boiled. She had gone back inside to walk through this large home. The residents of the farmhouse had left everything, including clothes—men's, women's, and children's. There were sheets, kitchen linens, and petticoats that could be made into bandages. The house was in working order, just empty. Sarah had hoped for a few days to prepare the house and start teaching about how to use plants and herbs before any sick or injured found them.

Ruby had the twins and Emma scrubbing and sweeping every corner of the house. Sarah knew the search for herbs, plants, and flowers must be started, even though it was early in the season. The supply that was taken from her root cellar would not last long.

Sarah had taken her books outside in an attempt to find what might be needed to heal. She walked into the woods behind the house in hopes of finding anything familiar. She was worried she would not recognize what could be right in front of her. Sarah had taken a moment, held her necklace, closed her eyes, and asked her mother for guidance. *Mother, help me. I need you.* When she opened her eyes, Leona was standing in front of her.

"I can help, Miss Sarah. I have found something," Leona told her.

Sarah followed Leona out of the stand of trees where she pointed to the ground.

"I found a root cellar just before you came out of the house."

Sarah and Leona entered the cellar.

Sarah was stunned at the enormity of this root cellar, three times the size of hers back home in Georgia. Sarah immediately recognized many of the roots and plants. Most were good, but there were many that had molded and couldn't be used. She found passionflower and black cherry. If there was a root cellar, then there would be a warming cupboard. There were some plants she did not recognize.

"I know these plants." Leona walked to each plant and called them by name. "This is wolfs bane, bush honeysuckle, orange root, boneset, and bee balm that can be used for measles;

bethroot helps in childbirth if the bleeding is too much. These two—flytrap and black haw—are used to help treat smallpox."

Sarah was curious about this teenager's knowledge of plants.

When Leona turned to look at Sarah, there were tears running down both sides of her face. "My maw was a healer. I helped her gather plants and watched her trade herbs and flowers with folks that came by our home," Leona told Sarah in a quiet voice.

Sarah put her arm around the young girl, and together they gathered what they could to take inside.

"I will check the books to see what else we can do with our newfound treasure. We'll explore the woods another day to see what is growing," Sarah told Leona.

Sarah became more curious about this family who lived here and why they left or what happened to them— questions she might never know the answers to, but she was grateful.

"Miss Sarah, I have been out searching deeper into the trees and close to the creek. There were some dandelions, sassafras, white willow, wintergreen, and witch hazel. There may be mayapple, I just haven't found it yet."

"It is wonderful what nature provides if you only know where to look. Leona, I want you to just call me Sarah."

Leona smiled, and they walked back to the house, aprons filled with what they could hold. When Sarah and Leona entered the house, they were assaulted with an odor Sarah knew only as death.

The house was now full of injured and sick people asking for help.

Ruby Belle walked up to Sarah and Leona.

"Where? How?" Sarah asked.

"Woman, I don't know, but it's time to help these poor souls," Ruby responded.

Sarah took all they had gathered from the cellar. She went to the kitchen and found the warming cupboard.

"Leona, I want you to go back to the trees and bring back some of the wintergreen you found, and hurry."

Leona ran out the back door to get what Sarah had requested.

"Emma, please take the twins and begin boiling water. Then go find clean sheets and start tearing them into bandages. Have Leona help you when she returns."

Sarah left the kitchen and went to the main room where she was shocked at the sight before her.

There were men with stumps covered in dirty bandages, sick children alone, women young and old sick and begging for help. The older men standing close to the door obviously had flux; several were shivering even though their faces were red and there was sweat on their brows.

No time, no time to teach. Sarah once again took the heart necklace in her hand and took command of the house and all therein like a general on a battlefield giving orders to soldiers.

"Sadie, Sallie, once you have finished helping Emma, I want you to take all the children to a room down the hall to check for pox and insects. Separate any child that may have a fever or cough."

"Yes, ma'am," they both said together.

The children huddled together in a corner, waiting for someone to help them. There were no tears or cries as they waited. Sarah recognized the sadness in their eyes. There would be no food or tea that could heal the injury or hurt they had in their small hearts.

"Maud, I want you to take anyone with flux out to the barn. Do not let anyone go near the pond or creek. Find a place behind the barn and have the men dig a deep hole and fill it halfway up with straw. We have to keep the water free from human waste."

"All y'all that has the flux or the quickstep come with me. And y'all better stay outta the water, ya hear me?" Maud announced sternly in her Texas accent.

Four women and about eight men moved quickly out the door with Maud.

"Ruby Belle, please take these women and check for injuries. Ask them what we can do for them and if they are able to help us. If they are well and sturdy, we could use their help. Anyone that is ill, we will tend to them," Sarah told Ruby.

"Sarah, girl, what are you thinking?" Ruby asked.

"I am thinking that we are going to need more help. If these women are from this area, they can help us find food and supplies that we will need in the days ahead."

"I hear you, woman," Ruby agreed, smiling. "Ladies, I am Ruby Belle. Let's go have a talk."

The rest of the women went with Ruby to the front porch.

Sarah could hear her booming voice asking, "And what's ails you today?"

The twins returned and took all the children to a bedroom on the first floor. Every child went without argument.

Sarah looked at the men with stumps. She could see maggots moving under the dirty and stinking dressings; many had fevers as she checked them quickly. There were at least three that would be dead within a few days if they were not treated now.

Emma walked into the main room and motioned for Sarah to come to the kitchen. Once they couldn't be heard by the sick in the main room, Emma took Sarah's hands.

"What are you going to do, Sarah?"

"I am going to see how many of these men I can save."

Chapter 12

SEVEN DAYS LATER AT THE HEALING HOUSE

Sarah and Ruby were drinking coffee in the kitchen, looking at the list of supplies that were quickly dwindling.

"Ruby, I don't know what we are going to do," Sarah told her.

"The Lord will help us."

"I hope He's listening, because we are going to need a miracle pretty soon."

"God listens, child, and He helps those in need," Ruby responded.

Maud came into the kitchen. "Sarah, I can't believe it, but all those folks in the barn are getting better, and some have gone on home," Maud stated proudly.

"That is wonderful. How do you feel? No flux?" Sarah inquired.

"No, I kept my distance and instructed them on what I wanted them to do. We couldn't save their clothes, so we burned them. Good thing there was some left here in this house. The hole they are using for an outhouse will be covered once the last one is well," Maud told Sarah.

"We are going to need more outhouses dug. I don't want anyone using the trees or bushes," Sarah told them. "What about the children?"

"They are all doing good," Ruby told her. "It was so sad to see them without their folks, but the girls said they had no spots on them—just dirty, hungry, and lost."

"That is one less thing to be worried about," Sarah said.

"What about the herbs?" Maud asked.

"What Leona and I found in the root cellar is unbelievable. We will be fine for a little while longer," Sarah said thankfully.

"What we need is food, bandages, and some soap," Ruby said.

The twins came into the kitchen. "Mother, there are some folks at the front door," Sallie said. "Sick?" Sarah asked.

"No, ma'am," Sadie responded. "They have brought stuff."

Ruby, Sarah, Maud, and the twins went to the front door.

An older woman who had been treated for the flux came forward and spoke for several men and women that were standing with sacks of food, chickens, and other supplies.

"My name is Edith Blake. We have come back to this healing house to thank you for what you and your ladies have done for us. We haven't had a healer in the area for a while. The woman and her family that lived here were killed." Edith didn't go into details. "Doc Bell left months ago. Said he was needed elsewhere. If you had not come when you did, many of us would be buried up the hill there. We ain't got much, but we feel that it ain't not proper to take and not give in return. We'd all be happy if you'd take what we brought as payment for your services.

Sarah started to cry.

Ruby Belle shouted, "God provides, yes, he does."

Maud and the twins took what had been offered to them inside the house.

"Miss Sarah," Edith continued. "Some of the ladies here and me would be ever thankful if you would let us come and help you with your healing of the sick. We don't know the art of healing like you, but we are willing to learn. The preacher's wife said she would take all the little ones 'cause they have the room to keep them."

"Thank you, all of you, and yes, we can use all the help you can give us," Sarah told them.

Emma came to the front door to see what all the excitement was about and to call Sarah upstairs.

"Sarah, I need you."

"Jim?" Sarah responded.

Emma nodded her head. "He's not good."

Sarah turned and went quickly upstairs to a room where she had separated all the men with the illness that sometimes came when wounds and amputations were not properly treated. The days were now warmer, so windows have been opened to help stay the smell of death that filled the room. Linens were changed each day, sprinkled with rose water, and wintergreen was placed in every room. The men were kept clean and well fed. Of the three that were so close to death, two survived and continued to improve every day. Jim was the last of the three. Sarah and the others had done all that had been within their power and knowledge. They kept him clean and comfortable, and waited.

Sarah knelt silently next to his bed, looking at his drawn face and sunken eyes. She noticed as she put a cool compress on his head that the color of his skin had turned a terrible shade of gray.

"Miss Sarah," Jim said.

"Be quiet and rest."

"Miss Sarah, I need you to write a letter to my folks," Jim begged her.

"You can tell them when you see them."

"You don't lie very well. I know I ain't going to make it, and I want them to know I love them, and I fought well," Jim told her.

Sarah found paper and a pencil from a small desk in the room. She listened to him and wrote all that he asked. He told her where his folks live.

"Miss Sarah, promise you'll see my folks get that letter."

"I promise with all that is in me. I will be sure they get this letter."

"Thank you, Miss Sarah. Thank you."

Jim then closed his eyes and went back to sleep.

Emma had returned upstairs to see if she could be of help to Sarah.

"Emma, please stay with him. Can you do that for me?"

"Yes, I'll do that, and I will stay until he passes." Jim would not last the night. Emma took Sarah's place and reached to change the compress only to discover he had already died. She covered his face with a blanket. Emma closed the door and followed after Sarah. There were men from the area that had volunteered to bury the dead, and today they would be needed.

Sarah touched Emma's hand and went downstairs with the letter. She placed it with others that had been left with the promise they would be delivered. They would be passed on to soldiers and folks to deliver for those men that would never go home.

Chapter 13

METHODIST CHURCH
WASHINGTON, NORTH CAROLINA
EARLY DAYS OF THE BATTLE

Mack had been watching soldiers and officers going in and out of the church. She could not be sure if this building held high-ranking officers. If so, there would be information she could obtain. She had found the makeshift hospital and helped herself to supplies. Mack was unable to locate Sarah before entering the city as a Union soldier, but she had heard about a healing house south of Greenville. Once she searched the church for information, she would leave and take what supplies she had borrowed to this healing house. The people there might have knowledge of Sarah. Mack had noticed several men in civilian clothing. She had asked about them and had been told they were war correspondents. Mack had no interest in them. She was, however, concerned when she saw the four renegades with whom she had shared a jug a while back.

Those bastards were talking with a tall man she had been told was a reporter. She couldn't take the chance these men would find her and question why she left them. When the night came, she would gather information and leave.

Samuel had finished the article on the battle in Washington, North Carolina. It was not a major battle, but even the smaller skirmishes would have a place in history.

He had planned later in the evening to start another part on his "The Women Who Travel in War" series. Samuel had decided to report on some of the physicians who were not much more than butchers. He had also seen these doctors degrade and complain about the nurses, who were trying to help and relieve the suffering of the wounded. Samuel had become a supporter of these women and their plight. He had seen the nurses questioned about their abilities and education, but never had he seen the doctors thank these women. These were the women who cleaned the sick and wounded, showed compassion, and never complained. They had little accommodations and were exposed equally to the weather conditions. Was there any difference in their care of these men than the care of a family member, male or female? Did these women stop feeling or caring just because these men were not family? Hard questions, but he would address them.

Samuel had been told about a group of southern women who had set up a healing house south of Greenville. This information came from four young soldiers who claimed to have been separated from their regiment and had come to serve their country. Since this house was not close to the battle going on in Washington, he would not be able to leave immediately. He intended to investigate and interview these southern women before he was sent on his next assignment. He had been interviewing northern nurses, and now there was an opportunity to see the other side of the war.

Samuel took his articles and placed them in his pouch. He knew there would be limited food in camp, but headed out for a meal and to see what information he could get from officers and soldiers, gathering letters in exchange for information.

Mack watched a man leave the church. The dark had become a friend and she slipped into the building unnoticed. She checked several beds and found a small table with a leather pouch. Mack took no time looking at the contents; she took the pouch and left. The borrowed items from the Union had been collected and packed on Grey. Mack silently left the city and headed toward the healing house and hopefully her friend Sarah.

⌒

Samuel returned to the church with numerous letters from soldiers. He had not been fortunate in obtaining any information about future battles. He lit the lamp and was concerned when he couldn't find his pouch. Samuel sat on his bed of straw and tried to think. Who could possibly want his stories? There is so much of my series in there—interviews, my thoughts, where I want to go next with the articles. At this point he couldn't do anything but try and remember what he had written and start over. He was upset that anyone would steal. He would look in the morning again for his pouch and report the theft to Brigadier General John G. Foster. Samuel must now rewrite his report on this battle. It would be a long night for him.

Chapter 14

April 1, 1863
West of Washington, North Carolina

Mack changed clothes and made good time getting away from Washington. She would sleep in a tree during the night with Grey hidden away but within the sound of her voice.

The next morning, Mack started her journey to the healing house with the borrowed supplies and a leather pouch she hoped contained battle plans. A light rain had started, but her journey would be an easy one. Ignored by Union and Confederate troops alike, Mack appeared to be a young boy going home. She came upon a group of injured soldiers. There was only a light mist now.

"Johnny Reb!" Mack shouted. "Where you headed?"

"To the healing house," the young man answered.

"Where?" Mack inquired. "Just around the bend, boy."

Mack kicked Grey into a full gallop and came upon a large home with men and women standing outside.

"She has to be here, she has to," Mack told Grey.

A woman stood outside talking to those who have come for help. Mack approached riding fast. Mack was loud, frantic. "Is there a healer nurse named Sarah Bowen here?" Mack asked.

The woman appeared stunned for a moment. "Yes, she is here. Are you hurt?"

"No, but I have supplies for her." Mack jumped off Grey. "I have information. It is important for everyone here. I have to see her. Please, where is she? Can you take me to her? Hurry, I have to see her," Mack begged.

"That won't be necessary," Sarah said.

Mack saw Sarah as she walked outside to see what all the shouting was about.

Mack ran up the steps, grabbing and hugging Sarah.

"I knew it was you. I knew it."

∾

Sarah took Mack inside, and they picked up where they left off the day she departed the Bowen farm.

"I have supplies, food, and I may have some information for the south," Mack rambled on so fast Sarah could hardly keep up. "When did you leave? How long? What about James?"

"Mack, slow down. One thing at a time," Sarah told her.

Over the next few hours, Sarah and Mack caught up on all that had happened since they both left the farm.

"How did you learn about this place?" Sarah asked.

"From four disgusting soldiers you had a run-in with on your way here. That is the other reason I am here, Sarah. Those men are in Washington and planning another visit. They want what they didn't get the first time," Mack told her.

"We are safe now. We have a lot of people around."

"Sarah, those men will not be so easily put off—they will come here."

Sarah ignored Mack's warning for the moment.

"And what about you? Night Walker?" Sarah asked. "You seem to have made quite a name for yourself since leaving Waynesboro. I hear your name everywhere."

Mack blushed. "Not my doing, but I have been of some help. James, how is he?" Mack attempted to get the focus off of herself.

"I guess he is fine. He left angry after reading your letter. I left with Ruby and these women before he came back. I am sure he is working the farm with Uncle Mike's help," Sarah reassured Mack and herself.

"Angry at me?" Mack asked.

"And me," Sarah told her.

"Did you explain?"

"James never gave me a chance. He saddled a horse and went to Uncle Mike's or maybe Uncle Earl's. I left before he came back. I left a letter explaining everything."

Mack smiled at her friend. "Well, let's hope by the time the war is over he isn't angry at either of us."

⌒

As the women came in to meet Sarah's friend, Mack decided to continue the deception and introduced herself as a boy. Introductions were made, and a simple explanation of their friendship given to the others that satisfied their curiosity. Mack returned to Grey, bringing medical supplies and food inside with thanks and gratitude. Mack took Grey to the barn and tended to her friend with hay, water, and a needed brushing.

When Mack returned to the kitchen, she was met by Ruby Belle.

"Young man," Ruby Belle began, "can we fix you something to eat?"

"Yes, ma'am," Mack responded. "Sarah, I could use my hair cut if you have time."

Sarah smiled and nodded her head. "I think there is a pair of shears here somewhere."

"Sarah, I need to talk to you alone. It is of a personal matter," Mack said. They walked out the back door away from the rest. "This is embarrassing."

"Mack, we have been through a lot. I consider you family," Sarah reassured her.

"It's my curse," Mack began. "Since I left Waynesboro, I haven't had my curse. I promise you I haven't been with no one. You know that?"

Sarah had heard of this before.

"Mack, when women are not properly eating and are worried, working like men, and exercising like men, sometimes their cycles become irregular or stop altogether. You have not had the same life since you left. I believe it will return, maybe when you are not running all over the country being a spy," Sarah laughed.

"Good, I was worried."

They returned inside, and Mack quickly became an extra hand, helping Sarah and the others to care for the sick and injured who continued to come. That evening Mack and Sarah sat down at the small kitchen table with the leather pouch taken from Washington. Mack had hoped this had vital information about upcoming battles; this would be a huge prize for the south.

Mack was disappointed when she began reading. She stood, knocking over the chair she was sitting in.

"These aren't worth a damn to me," Mack said, upset.

"When did you start swearing?"

"Sometimes I have to. I also spit, play cards, gamble, and smoke when it is necessary." Mack was embarrassed to confess to Sarah.

Sarah laughed and read over the articles about nurses."Mack, you have to return these."

"What? I can't go back there just for these."

"You must. This man is writing about the future of nursing and healing. He is telling a story that my mother told me would be told one day. That we, healers and nurses, would be important, that women could make a difference in the care of the sick, if given the knowledge and opportunity. You have to take these back. Promise me, Mack! It shouldn't be too difficult a job for the Night Walker."

Mack looked at her dearest friend and said, "I guess I can make a trip back. If you really feel this is important."

"It is," Sarah told her. "It is important for all of us that are trying to make a difference in this war and in the future of caring for the sick, for all of us who travel the land and leave our homes to care for others."

"I will take them back. I promise," Mack said.

"Mack, do you know the name of the man who has written these stories?" Sarah asked.

"No, but I will try to find out for you."

~

The next few days were pleasant. Mack had enjoyed being with her friend.

Ruby Belle had gotten directions to Chancellorsville from the locals. Mack listened to this conversation with some concern.

"Chancellorsville?" she asked.

"We need to get there fast but safely," Ruby told Mack.

Sarah entered the conversation. "Our job here is done. It's time to leave and go where we will be needed next."

"Why would you want to leave here? You and these ladies are making a big difference, and you're safe."

"Mack, we are going to be needed in battles to come. We have to travel to the next place. We have to find other nurses and hospitals where we can be of use."

Mack knew the next battle would be larger, more men, more sickness, and more danger to her friend.

"Sarah, the next battle is not going to be like this. You will not always have good water or a safe place to be. There will be horrible injuries, and more men will die. You and these ladies will not be able to save everyone."

"We will do all that we can. We have to try. You understand, don't you?" Sarah asked.

Mack lowered her head. It would do no good to argue with Sarah. "Please take care of yourself and be careful." Mack worried for her friend. They walked off together, away from the others.

"The Night Walker shouldn't worry about us," Sarah told her. "We will be fine."

"I will find you," Mack said.

"I am sure you will," Sarah said, hugging her friend.

"I'll head back to Washington with the pouch tomorrow morning."

"We will be leaving in a couple of days."

Maud called for Sarah, "Have you seen Leona?"

Sarah and Mack walked back inside the house. "No, I sent her out to look for plants that we can take with us," Sarah told Maud.

"How long has she been gone?" Mack asked.

Sarah looked outside. "I sent her out this morning. That was several hours ago."

Mack took her knife out of the sheath as she ran out the back door and into the trees to look for Leona. They came back, they came back.

Sarah called for the others. Ruby and the rest of the women followed Sarah toward the trees. Mack was quick and headed deep into the trees, knowing this scum would want a place where no one could hear Leona scream.

Mack could hear the others calling Leona's name—no response. Mack headed to the creek where it ran hard. This was where she found Leona, facedown, blood running down both of her legs, dress all but gone. Mack kneeled down and turned her over. Her face was bruised and swollen.

"Leona, it's Mack, can you hear me?" She checked to make sure Leona was breathing.

Mack called out. "I found her!"

Sarah and Ruby Belle were the next to arrive.

"Mack, please tell me she is alive," Sarah pleaded.

"Yes."

"Maud!" Ruby bellowed out. "We need blankets. Hurry!"

"My fault, it's my fault, Mack. I should have listened to you," Sarah cried. She then kneeled and checked Leona's injuries. "I should have sent someone with her to protect her."

"They would be dead, Sarah. Those bastards wouldn't let anyone stop them from getting what they wanted." Mack's anger was building.

Leona was carried back to the house where her injuries were attended, but they would have to see what damage had been done to her mind. Sarah refused to leave her bedside. She knew the assault could lead to a pregnancy.

The next morning the women's trip to Chancellorsville was delayed, as Leona's welfare came first.

Mack had saddled Grey. We will find them. She led him out to the front of the house. Mack went in to find Sarah and to check on Leona.

Mack silently entered the room where Sarah continued her vigil at Leona's bedside. "How is she?" Mack inquired.

"She hasn't spoken, opened her eyes, or moved since we brought her back to the house," Sarah told her.

"Sarah, I have to go. There are things I must do and papers to return."

"I know." Sarah stood and hugged Mack. "Take care, twig."

"You and these ladies must be careful once you leave here. Take no chances," Mack told her.

At that moment, Leona reached out and took Sarah's hand. "Water."

Chapter 15

METHODIST CHURCH
UNION TROOPS LEAVING WASHINGTON,
NORTH CAROLINA

Night had come, and Samuel had made his way back to the church to finish packing his things and prepare to leave. He had received word he would be heading to Chancellorsville. His desire to interview the women at the healing house would have to wait. He had stayed longer in Washington than he had planned, due to the theft of his papers.

Samuel walked toward his bed when he became aware that someone else stood in the darkness with him.

"Who's there? Can I help you with something?" Samuel asked, thinking another soldier had come to ask him to mail a letter back home.

"I have something that belongs to you, Samuel White." The voice was low, almost whispering. From the shadows, a small hand extended his pouch to him.

At that moment, Samuel knew he was in the presence of the Night Walker.

Samuel could not believe what was happening. His papers had been returned, undamaged, by the very person he had hoped to find. How could he approach this person? What could he say to get information that would lead to an exclusive interview?

"These are of no value to me, Mr. White. If it had been up to me, I would have used them for kindling," the Night Walker told him, staying in the shadows. "They are, however, important to someone very special to me. She is a friend who heals, who believes in what you are writing. She made me bring them back so that you can finish the articles about nurses."

Samuel was surprised that the Night Walker had taken the time to read his articles, but intrigued about this friend, the healer. A woman that could influence someone to take a chance of being captured or killed to return his stories would be someone he would want to interview.

"How do you know my name?" Samuel asked.

"People are eager to talk when you have something to trade."

"What did you trade to get my name and information? How did you know I was still in camp?"

"A few fresh biscuits and some peach jam." The Night Walker said. "Your stature is not easily ignored."

Samuel was somewhat disappointed he did not fetch a higher price, but happy to have his papers returned.

"And who is this friend that sent you back into danger?" Samuel asked.

Mack ignored the question about Sarah; she was not going to reveal any name to this man. The safety of her friends came first.

He lit a lamp and then looked toward the darkness. "May I? What you have to say is important and needs to be written."

"I don't want it in my face or I will leave," the voice said firmly.

"I promise. Only so that I can see to write," Samuel replied.

Samuel saw the Night Walker's small stature, which made sense to him. This had been how he was able to come and go unnoticed. Dark clothing from head to foot, Samuel bet he had a Union uniform.

"Please tell me about yourself and your friend. What did you say your friend's name was?" Samuel asked.

"I am not inclined to give you a name. Trust is very important to me, and you have not earned that at this point. All you need to know is that she has traveled far from her home to help in this war."

Samuel was impressed. "You are correct. Trust is very important, and I will attempt to gain yours. Can you tell me what makes this friend of yours so special?"

Samuel listened as the Night Walker described his friend the healer. He discovered that the nurses and healers of the south were confronted with the same horrors as those in the north.

The Night Walker told Samuel how important healing with nature was to his friend, as well as the caring and kindness she showed to everyone, regardless of the color of their skin.

"This woman treats slaves?" Samuel asked.

"She treats everyone and was one of the women at the healing house south of Greenville." Mack could not believe she had been so careless to give away Sarah's location, but hoped she and the others would be gone if this man chose to look for her.

"Your friend was at the healing house?"

"Yes. She was when I left."

"I have to find her and speak to her," Samuel responded.

"She and the other nurses are kind and generous. I will expect you to be a man of honor."

"I assure you my interest will be to gather information for my stories. I will remain a gentleman at all times, you have my word. Do you think she might still be there?"

"She may be leaving with the nurses that are headed to the next battle." The voice was hurried. Samuel looked out the window. Daylight would be coming soon.

"I must go," the Night Walker stated.

"Wait, I have so much to ask you. Your story is important." Samuel tried to play to the young man.

"I am of no importance...I am only a messenger."

Samuel looked at the notes he had made, and when he looked up to ask another question, he realized The Night Walker had gone. He left without a sound, not even a board creaking. How did he do that? It wasn't possible to leave and not be heard. But he had.

⌒

Mack made her way in the darkness to Grey. She patted her friend and told him, "We have something that needs to be tended to, Grey. We have a wrong that must be made right."

Mack took a few minutes to check the pouches she had taken from Sarah's root cellar in Georgia that contained herbs: pokeberry, poison hemlock, and moonseed. Sarah's books showed her how to store them, their uses, and how they were to be handled. Sarah had marked large letters on all of these that said DO NOT USE. Mack had made her own notes inside the cover of Jane Eyre before leaving Waynesboro.

While Mack was at the healing house, Leona had showed her yellow jasmine in the cellar.

"I don't understand why this is here," Leona told Mack. "This can kill you."

While they were outside, Leona had taken her to a bush called oleander. "You need to be careful of this plant," Leona warned. "It will kill animal and human alike. All parts of this are deadly—the flowers when they bloom, sap, seeds, and just ten to twenty leaves, green or dry, can kill a full-grown man."

Mack had reentered the cellar that same day and taken the yellow jasmine. She stopped shortly after leaving the healing house and carefully pulled enough leaves from the oleander bush to kill four men. She had taken the time to learn the safe way to touch and mix these plants. A little something that would take care of her problems once she found them. Mack swung into the saddle and, once again, left Washington unnoticed.

Chapter 16

HEALING HOUSE
THREE DAYS AFTER ATTACK

Sarah, I am not going to stay here," Leona said while she sat with the rest of the women in the back of the wagon."You are the only family I have. I can't lose you, too." She began to cry.

"Ruby, tell her she will heal better here. The trip will be long and difficult for her." Sarah looked for help and at the bruises that marked Leona's face and the swelling on her left eye and upper lip. The constant cool compresses of witch hazel had taken away the majority of the swelling, but the bruises were a reminder at this moment that Sarah could not protect her.

Leona saw the sadness in Sarah's face and her worry for the days ahead.

"Sarah, you have to stop blaming yourself for what happened. It wasn't your fault. Please, please don't leave me behind."

"Sarah, we talked this over last night," Sadie started.

"We can't leave her, Miss Sarah. Please," Sallie begged.

Maud, Ruby, and Emma all nodded in agreement.

Sarah knew in her heart that Emma should not go either. Emma did not eat enough, had not gained enough weight or rested like Sarah had instructed. She had become concerned over the welfare of the baby and checked every few days for movement. Emma's only interest had been Leonard. She neglected her own needs and those of her unborn child.

"Leona is stronger than you give her credit for," Ruby told Sarah and hugged her.

"Leona, you promise to rest until I think you're ready to help?" Sarah asked.

"Until you say so, I promise." Leona crossed her heart.

"Then I guess the only thing left to do is go," Sarah told everyone.

The women laughed and cheered as Sarah turned to make one last trip into the healing house, which would be left in the good hands of Edith and the women of the area.

"Miss Sarah, God bless you, and may he keep all of you ladies safe." Edith reached out for Sarah.

"I have left instructions, herbs—" Sarah started.

"Get on, girl. We will be fine. Go on now before you make me cry." Edith shooed at Sarah with her apron. "You are gonna lose the sun if you don't go."

"The letters.. .don't forget the letters," Sarah reminded her.

"Girl, they are already gone. Don't you worry about a thing," Edith smiled.

Sarah left the house and went to join her friends who were waiting.

Ruby helped Sarah up to the seat with her. Sarah waved good-bye to the friends they had made at the healing house.

"Ladies, it will take about twelve days of traveling to get to Chancellorsville," Ruby said.

Sarah looked down to see Ruby's rifle within reach. She had watched Maud and Ruby practice firing their guns behind the barn several times since Leona was attacked. The guns had been cleaned and reloaded, and several boxes of ammunition obtained for their trip. Food and medical supplies were restocked in the wagon, along with fresh water. Ruby had been very sparing with the moonshine, so they had plenty.

"No one goes anywhere alone—even to relieve themselves," Ruby informed them.

Sarah continued to care for Leona as a pregnancy could have occurred from the attack. Sarah would never be able to live with herself if that happened.

Leona moved up close to Sarah. "Thank you, Sarah, for not leaving me."

Sarah held Leona's hand and looked down the road. Decisions to be made in the future may not be so easy.

"Ruby, please try and find a church tonight. I want to make sure we are all safe, out of the weather, and together," Sarah requested.

"I'll do my best, girl. I'll do my best."

Chapter 17

THE ROAD TO THE HEALING HOUSE
APRIL 20, 1863

Samuel had made the decision to go toward Greenville and the healing house. He hoped that the southern healer would still be there along with the rest of the women traveling together. Now he had something to really write about: southern nurses and the Night Walker all drawn together. This healer would know the real name of this elusive spy.

Samuel was worried about finding the house, but he only had to follow the sick and injured. He had found a Confederate soldier, unable to walk further, along the side of the road. He stopped and put this man on his mount and then walked the last two miles to the healing house. Several women saw Samuel coming down the road with the injured soldier and came to assist. They asked so many questions about this soldier's injury: how long he was on the side of the road, when he last had something to eat or drink. Samuel had to stop them.

"Ladies, you'll have to get those answers from this man. I simply found him and brought him here."

They helped Samuel take the man off his horse and into the home. Samuel watched an older woman walk toward him.

"Young man, are you injured or ill?" she asked.

"No, ma'am. I found that man and couldn't leave him on the roadside," Samuel told her.

"All are welcome here, even the Yankees, as long as they behave themselves. My name is Edith Blake."

"Thank you. I am Samuel White with the Franklin Weekly from New York. I am looking for a southern healer and the nurses with her. I am writing stories about nurses on both sides of the war."

"Lord above! She and them other angels left several days ago heading for Chancellorsville," Edith said. "Goodness, young man, I hope you have a lot of paper in that pouch. That woman is a breath of fresh air in all that is bad in the world at this moment."

Samuel was disappointed he had missed them. "Was there a young boy here with her, about fourteen or fifteen years old?" he asked.

"You mean Mack?"

"Mack? Is that his name?" Samuel inquired.

"Yes, Mack was here for a short time. Sweet boy. He and Sarah seem to be very close. He didn't really tell us much and neither did Sarah. Those of us here didn't ask. It isn't polite to intrude on folks' private talk, you know?" Edith paused. "Would you break bread with us and spend the night, Samuel?"

"Yes, I believe I will. Did you say Sarah?" Samuel asked.

"Why, yes, I did. Sarah Bowen. I believe she was from Georgia."

Samuel took a moment to digest all the information he had just been given. The Night Walker and Sarah were friends, his childhood friend had been within a day's ride of him, and now she was gone, headed for Chancellorsville. He should leave now and attempt to find Sarah, but there was a story here, one that needed to be documented. He decided to stay, listen, and learn about his childhood friend. He would ask about the strength of these women who traveled to war. For the rest of the day and into the night, Samuel followed Edith through the house. He observed these women put into practice what Sarah had taught them in a short period of time.

"Did any of Sarah's patients die?" Samuel asked.

Edith stopped and wiped her eyes. "There was a young boy here. His arm had been injured, and was cut off by some darn fool doctor. By the time he got here, there was green fluid running out of it, bugs crawling in the wound. He was in a bad way." She shivered just to think about it. "He was too far gone. That girl and the others cleaned him, his wound, used several different herbs and poultices to try and save that young man. They all took turns sitting up with him throughout the long nights, but in the end, all they could do was give him God's peace. The day he passed, he called Sarah to write a letter to his folks," Edith sniffed."His name was Jim. He's buried up the hill there."

Samuel sat up past midnight writing about what he had seen and been told by Edith. Samuel's next featured article would read: "The Women Who Work with Nature to Heal." He would leave in the morning and try to catch up with Sarah.

Chapter 18

RALEIGH, NORTH CAROLINA
APRIL 21, 1863

It had been only a few days since Mack left Samuel and began her search for justice for Leona. She tracked the four back to Greenville, then to Raleigh. She went into town late, hoping to find them all together. Mack passed a saloon and heard a familiar voice coming out the door. It was the oldest of the group.

"Come on, you bastards. We gotta get going," the oldest one screamed.

"We're heading to Mississippi instead of going north to Chancellorsville," the fat one told him, pointing to his pock-marked friend. He knew this could lead to a beating for not following orders.

"Fine. When we catch back up with them whores from that house, I am taking that blonde Sarah. I won't waste my time on no kid again," the tall one said, as he reached for his gun.

They all laughed and continued their comments on the fun they all had with Leona.

"You two are worthless anyway. Get on, and don't come crawling back begging to join up with the two of us again," the oldest told them.

Mack stood in the shadows and listened. The men decided to split up, which would make Mack's job easier. She followed in the blackness of the night, observing each man. She watched as they separated and left town. Mack went to the back of the saloon and crawled through an open window. She disappeared out the window with two bottles of whiskey.

Grey waited quietly as Mack approached. She had given the ones going to Mississippi a wide berth. It was now time to follow. She would catch up with the other two in Chancellorsville where she had something special planned for them.

Chapter 19

THE ROAD TO CHANCELLORSVILLE

The sun shining on Sarah's face was welcomed. The warmth was wonderful after the cooler weather they had encountered since leaving Georgia. There were leaves on trees, and the flowers had begun to bloom in some of the areas they had traveled.

Ruby had been good at finding churches or folks that would allow them to stay in a barn or shed overnight. As Leona continued to heal, she talked about what happened to her. Sarah had been worried that she would hold all the bad inside. Leona came to Sarah the second night they were on the road.

"Sarah, my maw told me that when bad things happen to a person, whether it be illness, death, or a happening beyond our control, it is best to empty the heart of all the bad, heal the hurt, and mend the soul. I need to heal my body and my soul. I need to talk to all of you."

What an amazing child to have gone through so much in her young life. Ruby Belle was right about Leona being stronger than I thought.

"Sarah, where are your thoughts, woman?" Ruby nudged her arm.

"Just thinking and enjoying the sunshine," Sarah responded.

"There is a lake ahead of us. I hope we can find some good folks along there that will let us stop for the night," Ruby continued.

"We need to fill the barrels, and I need to look for plants. What I really want is to clean myself and change clothes." Sarah's green day wrapper was soiled and bloodstained. "I only have this and my blue one. I gave the brown one away at the healing house."

"Ruby Belle, stop the wagon," Maud called from the back. "Sarah, we have a problem."

Ruby pulled the wagon to a stop. Sarah jumped down and ran to where Emma was lying on a quilt.

"It's wet," Maud told Sarah.

"It's too soon. Is my baby going to die?" Emma's face was pale.

"I don't know. I wish I did, but I just don't know," Sarah told her.

Sarah looked at the rest of the faces in the wagon. She saw only love and concern for their friend.

"Ruby, how far are we from the lake?" Sarah asked.

"Nightfall, best I can tell."

"We need to go and find a place to stop. I don't want to be on the road should this baby decide to come." Sarah stayed in the back of the wagon with Emma. Fluid continued to come. Sarah felt for movement. There was none. This was a secret she kept to herself for the moment.

∾

They arrived in a place called Gaston, North Carolina. Those last few miles before arriving in town had seemed to be the longest. Emma was beginning to have pain, but not the type Sarah had expected.

The minister of the Baptist church and his wife agreed to let them stay in their home.

"You and your ladies are welcome here," Pastor Allen told them.

"What can I do to help you ladies?" Barbara, his wife, asked.

"Mrs. Allen, one of our women is having birthing pains. Her water has broken," Sarah explained. "The baby is early, and I am concerned about both of them."

"We will do whatever we can to help," Barbara said.

"At this moment, pray," Sarah told her.

Ruby and Maud settled the horses for the night. Sadie, Sallie, and Leona made beds for themselves in the barn.

"Mrs. Allen," Sarah started.

"Sarah, please call me Barbara."

"Barbara, can you stay with Emma for a few minutes? I need to check on the girls in the barn."

Sarah went to the kitchen and made tea for Leona—a tea she had made every day since they left the healing house. Sarah went out to the barn and checked on everyone. She handed the tea to Leona, who drank it without question.

"Ruby, will they be all right for the night out here?" Sarah asked.

"I think so, woman. Why?"

Sarah had Ruby and Maud follow her outside the barn, away from the others.

"I may need you and Maud throughout the night to help with Emma." Sarah looked at the ground, not wanting to face what she already knew was going to happen. "I believe that Emma's baby has died."

"No, Sarah, please tell us you're wrong," Maud begged.

"Even if I am wrong, this baby is early and could be small," Sarah said, trying to prepare them. "I am going to need both of you to help me tonight."

"Girl, anything. You know we will do whatever you need," Ruby told her.

"We can take turns watching over the younger ones outside," Maud said.

Sarah made a list of what she would need during the night: black cherry, partridge berry, passionflower, chokecherry juice, and valerian. She wasn't sure the partridge berry would help, since it should be used weeks before birthing began.

Barbara had made tea and food for Sarah and her ladies. Maud returned with Sarah and took the food out to the barn for the girls. She would stay until they were asleep and take first watch.

"You ladies will be safe here," Barbara began. "We have had no molestation of our women by either side."

"We have," Sarah responded. "My reasoning to keep them outside is due to my concerns for Emma and her child. You and your husband are more than kind. I must be honest with you. Emma has not been well with her pregnancy. I have worried since the first day I met her. She has not gained weight, and she pushed herself to help when she should have been resting. She is alone, and this child is her hope for a love that cannot be at the present."

Barbara reached out and touched Sarah's hand.

"He will give you all the strength you need to get you through this."

"Barbara, I mean no disrespect, but it's not me that will need God's strength. It will be that young woman in there that is about to lose her baby."

Chapter 20

TENNESSEE/NORTH CAROLINA BORDER

Mack had taken the two horses with their supplies and walked back to where Grey waited in the trees. She took the Union uniform off once more and replaced it with the dark clothing that shielded and protected her in the night.

She tied the two horses behind Grey. Grey looked at her as she swung into the saddle.

"They won't need them anymore. We will drop them off at the first Confederate camp we come to," Mack told Grey.

Once again the Night Walker disappeared into the darkness. The bodies she left behind would just be two more casualties of the war. The empty whiskey bottles were buried, so no innocent would be tempted to use them.

Two down, two to go...

Chapter 21

Ruby Belle and Maud were loading some supplies that Barbara had given them to make their journey a little easier. Pastor Allen had helped Sadie and Sallie with fresh water the day before.

Sarah stood with Leona inside the Allen home, listening to what Barbara Allen had to say.

"Sarah, the mind will take a tragedy and hide it away until it can face the truth. Emma has done this with the loss of her baby. She has no husband to hold onto, unsure if he is alive, and to admit that this child is not alive is too much for her mind. Emma must have something real in her life, and at the moment, it is this child. She will be fine here with us. I have seen this before in our community—a melancholy that affects the mind as well as the body."

"Barbara, please look at this. Emma just gave it to me." Sarah handed Barbara a piece of paper.

Private Leonard Williams, Georgia 53rd Leonard,

Our daughter is born. I have named her Ruth after your mother. We are waiting for you in Gaston, North Carolina, with Pastor and Mrs. Allen. Please come soon.

Our love,

Emma and Ruth

Barbara handed the letter back to Sarah.

"Keep it with you. Maybe you will find this young man and can tell him what has happened here. He will need to know," Barbara said.

Ruby Belle came inside the house. "It's time to go, Sarah." Ruby placed her strong hands on Sarah's shoulders. "We are going to have to push hard over the next few days to get to Chancellorsville."

"I know. I'm ready."

Leona took Sarah's hand, and they walked to the wagon.

"Sarah! Sarah, thank you, my friend! Ruth and I will be here waiting for Leonard," Emma shouted to her.

As Ruby turned the team to leave Gaston, they watched Barbara, Pastor Allen, and Emma holding her dead baby, waving good-bye.

Chapter 22

GASTON, NORTH CAROLINA
SUNDAY MORNING

Samuel had been crossing back and forth between enemy lines, collecting stories as he searched for Sarah and the Night Walker. This decision to not stay on the Union side had given him more information about the Night Walker than he could have ever hoped to obtain through gossip and speculation in northern campsites. It had almost gotten him shot on more than one occasion. The papers he carried for the Weekly had been his so-called saving grace. Samuel had hoped he would have found the ladies traveling to Chancellorsville, but he seemed to have missed them so far. He had two stories that would continue for the rest of the war. One had become very personal; the other about the Night Walker would be amazing.

The weather continued to improve along with Samuel's spirit and enthusiasm.

It was Sunday morning when he rode into Gaston, North Carolina, and up to the Baptist church, where he heard singing. He had never been a religious man, but today he felt a pull, a need to give thanks for his life and luck.

Samuel entered the church and sat in the back. He listened to the sermon on giving help to those in need and loving one another. The pastor began to tell about a group of women that had traveled through on their way to help the sick and wounded. Samuel suddenly sat up and realized Sarah had been here. He couldn't believe he had missed her again. There must be a story here, and hopefully the pastor would share it with me.

After services, Samuel introduced himself to the pastor and asked if he could talk with him about these ladies.

"Barbara," the pastor called to his wife. "Meet Samuel White of the Franklin Weekly, all the way from New York."

Two women walked up. The younger woman was holding a blanket with a doll wrapped in it.

"This is Ruth. She is three days old," the young woman told Samuel. Samuel looked at Barbara Allen, puzzled.

"Come, Emma." Barbara put her arm around the woman. "Mr. White, will you join us for dinner? I would enjoy talking to you about many things that have happened to us in the past few days."

"If you have room at your table, I would be honored."

"There is always room for one more in our home, Samuel. Please come. I will show you the way," Pastor Allen said.

The afternoon progressed into evening, and Samuel had not enjoyed a meal like this since leaving New York.

"Samuel, will you have another piece of pie?" Barbara asked.

"No, I just do not have any room left to put another piece of pie. Thank you for a wonderful meal. I would like to talk with both of you if this is a good time." He took out his writing pad and pencil.

Barbara looked nervously at her husband.

"Emma, let's take Ruth outside for a walk," Pastor Allen told her. He stood, smiled, and they left the house.

Once Emma and Pastor Allen had left, Samuel looked at Barbara Allen.

"What happened to Emma?" Samuel asked.

Barbara told him of the tragedy that had befallen her and the love of six others that allowed them to leave her in the Allen's' care.

"The doll?" Samuel inquired.

"It is my replacement for a child that needed to be blessed and buried. It is my hope to bring Emma back to all that has happened to her, but in time and slowly." Barbara stopped their conversation as her husband and Emma returned.

"Samuel, will you stay the night with us?" Pastor Allen asked.

"Pastor, I feel as though I need to travel on, but there is a story here I need to finish. Yes, I will stay the night."

Pastor Allen watched his wife take Emma to her room. "Samuel, you are correct. There is a story here. Men are not the only ones affected in this war. We all suffer. That is a story all of us need to know."

Samuel smiled and knew the pastor was right about telling Emma's story. Samuel finished it just before midnight. He found the comfort of a real bed inviting and quickly went to sleep. The next thing he remembered was Pastor Allen calling him to breakfast.

"Samuel, where will you go next?" Barbara asked.

"I must find Sarah—"

"Sarah, my friend, Sarah? Is she here? Have you seen her?" Emma asked Samuel.

"No, Emma. I am trying to find her."

"Tell Sarah...tell her my baby, my Ruth, we.. .we need..." she started to cry.

Barbara stood and wrapped her arms around Emma. "It will be fine. Let's go check on Ruth."

Samuel bowed his head. "This is heartbreaking," he told the pastor.

"Can I get you anything before you continue on your journey?" Pastor Allen asked.

"A little coffee, if you have it. I'll be happy to pay."

"No, you will not pay us," Barbara told him. "Emma is resting. Sometimes she knows the baby is dead. It will just take time to heal. We have love to spare." Barbara walked over and took her husband's hand. "I will get your coffee while you get ready to leave. Emma will want to say good-bye, too."

Pastor Allen, Barbara, and Emma walked outside to see Samuel on his way and give any last directions he might need. As he got on his horse, the pastor said, "Samuel, I feel a blessing would be appropriate at the start of a journey."

"I would be honored to have your blessing. Thank you."

"The Lord bless and keep you. May He shine His love on you always," Pastor Allen finished.

"Take care of yourself, young man. You will always be welcome in our home," Barbara told Samuel.

"Tell Sarah I miss her very much," Emma said.

"What else should I tell Sarah and the others should I find them?" Samuel asked Barbara.

"Time, love, and prayer," Barbara told him. "Sarah will understand."

Samuel nodded his head and left Gaston, hoping to make up for lost time.

Chapter 23

Two Days Later

Emma woke in the night to the cries of a baby. "Ruth? Where is my baby? Who has taken my baby?" she whispered.

Emma left the Allen's' home in her nightgown to go and look for the baby that had been stolen from her.

"I have to find her. What will Leonard say if I let someone steal our baby? He won't love me. He will leave me," she said to no one.

She ran, crying, to where the road ended and the water began. The cries became louder and more urgent as Emma looked across the water."Ruth, Ruth! Mommy is here. Don't cry. Mommy is here."

Chapter 24

Mack had found the last of the four renegades. They had attached themselves to the least dangerous work in camp. These men had placed themselves away from any chance they would be involved in actual fighting by unloading supplies that had arrived for the Sanitation Commission in preparation for the battle ahead. She had followed them for hours, learning their routine, where they slept, and when they ate.

Mack had planned this since she left the healing house. She dressed as a woman with a bonnet covering most of her face. Entering the camp with other women and children was easier than using her Union uniform. She blended into camp life with the others. Mack had no interest in appropriating supplies at this time. She was here for one purpose only.

As evening came, Mack found a meal cooking for the women and children. She obtained two extra bowls and headed to the medical tents to find the rabble. Inside the pocket of her apron was the pouch that contained what would be needed to finish a personal promise. She entered and found the last of Leona's attackers helping themselves to medicinal alcohol.

"What are you looking at, brat?" the oldest one said.

"I didn't know there were little girls in camp," the tall one told Mack and laughed.

"My maw is cooking and helping to get ready for the wounded. She made soup and had been watching you two working hard all day. She sent me to find and feed you," Mack responded.

"Hot biscuits, too?" the oldest looked at Mack, salivating over her and the food.

"Yes, sir." Mack was aware the older one was staring, so she lowered her head, refusing to look at them straight on. "My maw used the last of the flour she brought with her to make these here biscuits," Mack told them.

"Guess we better eat while this is hot," the tall one told his friend.

"If it ain't any good, we can wash it down with the liquor," the oldest one laughed.

"Get, girl, and don't you tell anyone where you found us," the tall one warned Mack. "Not even your maw."

"No, sir, I won't," she told them. Mack turned and skipped out of the tent like a child, turning one last time to watch as both men dug greedily into the bowls of soup. They used the biscuits to sop up what couldn't be gotten with a spoon.

Mack changed back into her Union uniform in the darkest part of night. She returned to the tent just before dawn, took the bowls, and discarded them. Mack made sure there would never be any further signs of life from these men. They must look as if they had been attacked and killed in a fight with the enemy, not poisoned. When she was finished, she sheathed her knife and left them behind the stacks of supplies where she had found them earlier in the evening.

Mack smiled and left Savage Station. She headed toward the rest of the Union armies to obtain information for the south, hopeful that she would find Sarah. There would always be another battle ahead of them.

Chapter 25

GEORGIA 51ST AND 53RD TURNPIKE, MAY 1

Leonard, keep your head down or some Yankee will take it off your shoulders," the loud voice of the lieutenant called out to this young private.

"Yes, sir," Leonard responded. "Sir, who was that civilian you were talking to?"

"He said he was a reporter from New York. Damn fool almost got himself shot riding up on us like he did," the lieutenant said.

"What did he want?" Leonard asked.

"General Lee. Then told me he needs to report on both sides of this war," the lieutenant told him.

"You weren't gone very long. Did General Lee agree to see him?" Leonard asked.

"General Lee agreed to see him and give him an interview and said he could stay as long as he stayed off the battlefield. I couldn't believe it.

"Lieutenant, how long do you think we will be here, sir?"

"As long as it takes, Private. As long as it takes," the lieutenant told him as he looked at the red heart he held in his hand.

Samuel's luck continued as he sat with General Lee asking questions and receiving the answers in a straightforward manner. General Lee had impressed Samuel, along with the officers who surrounded this man. Samuel expressed his gratitude to the general.

"General Lee, I would like to give my appreciation to one of your lieutenants. He stopped his men from killing me as I rode into Confederate lines."

"Do you know this man's name?" one of the officers asked.

"No, but he is attached to the Georgia 53rd," Samuel answered.

"I will attempt to get his name for you, while you are our guest," General Lee told him.

Samuel regretted that he hadn't gotten the lieutenant's name, but he would never forget the man's face when he handed him the red heart he had dropped. It must have been of great importance to him.

Another man of importance, Major General Jackson, was on Samuel's list to interview and follow over the next few days. He would also be looking for Mack. Should the Night Walker be found, Samuel would be able to obtain a more in-depth view of this incredible boy. He had inquired about this spy, but the boy seemed to be an enigma with his own people. The officers did not have much information on him either. The Night Walker seemed to be the Confederates' best kept secret, even among themselves.

He finished his interviews and had been introduced to one of Major General Jackson's aides, whom he would attach himself to over the next few days. Samuel was taken to an area where he would be safe and could observe. Samuel became frustrated with standing back and watching the battles from a distance. He needed to get closer to the actual fighting, to be able to experience firsthand what these men faced in battle.

He took the time in which he had been safely put away from the fight to refine his interview with General Lee. He dug through his pouch to find the notes taken at Gaston. Samuel's next article in "The Women Who Travel in War" series would be Emma's story. It would be called "Their Sacrifices."

The article he had started on The Night Walker might be a story with no ending.

Chapter 26

Sarah and the women she now considered friends had finally found the area called the Wilderness Tavern—a hospital set up by the Confederates where nurses were needed.

"RUBY BELLE! What in heaven's name are you doing here?" a loud voice turned the heads of all of the women who had just crawled out of the wagon.

"Mollie? Mollie Mae?" Ruby said.

Ruby walked to a woman that could have been her sister. The two hugged and laughed, but then ducked as gunfire began. "We should have been here days ago, but life does not always agree with what we plan," Ruby told Mollie.

"I wasn't expecting any extra help, so this is a blessing. I am happy to have you and your friends. Come with me, and I will get a place that is safe for you and your ladies," Mollie said.

Sarah looked around at the scene before her. There were men lying in filth—some dead, many dying. Thankfully the weather improved daily, which meant there would be flowers, plants, and maybe honey. She would take Leona and look for plants once they had settled. Sarah had noticed the damage from artillery shells; too many men tromping down the very thing that might save their lives. This might not be as easy as she had hoped.

"There may not be all the comforts of home, but I can offer you food and shelter," Mollie told them.

"We will be fine, Mollie. Tell us where we are needed," Ruby told her.

"Settle in and then we will talk." She took them to an area where the horses could be kept, and there was some shelter for them should it rain.

"Thank you, Mollie. Ladies, time to unload. This is home for a while," Ruby told them.

"Ruby, I take it by your reaction to Mollie that you two are friends," Maud said.

"Mollie and I go back more years than I want to admit to, and maybe one day I will tell you ladies a story about two girls that ran away together," Ruby laughed and walked away for a moment.

"Leona, I you want you to come with me," Sarah said. "We have plants and flowers to locate before dark."

Leona leaned into Sarah.

"I need supplies. My cycle has come early."

Sarah nodded her head.

"Wait a minute. You'll need this," Maud said, handing Sarah a gun. "It's loaded and ready to fire. Aim low. It has a little kick to it."

"I hope we won't need it," Sarah told her and put the gun in her dress pocket.

"Don't be gone long, ya hear? I'll come looking for y'all if you're not back by dusk," Maud told them.

"We won't be gone that long."

"Sarah, Mollie wants us all to meet at the wagon after dinner. She has instructions and items to give us. She said we will need them in the field," Maud continued talking as the two walked off.

Sarah waved as she and Leona disappeared into the trees.

~

"Maud, do you think giving Sarah that gun is a good idea?" Ruby asked.

"Sarah can shoot straight and true as you or I."

"How do you know that?" Ruby asked.

"Once Leona began to talk after the attack, Sarah had Sadie and Sallie watch over Leona one afternoon. I followed Sarah to the back of the barn and watched her for over an hour shoot both gun and rifle. She never missed once."

"That makes me feel better then."

"Girls, get those supplies out of the wagon! Don't make me tell you two again," Ruby yelled to the twins.

"Yes, ma'am," they responded.

"What about the moon?" Sadie started.

"Sadie, we don't talk about that right now. That is for emergencies, and from what I have seen, there will be plenty of those here," Ruby told her.

"Maw, where do you want me to put Sarah's supplies?" Sallie asked.

"Keep those hid for now, girl. I am not sure these docs are going to appreciate her the way we do."

~

Samuel had been keeping up as closely as possible to Major General Jackson. He made notes and sketches of what he had seen with all the movement of troops from both sides.

One of Jackson's aides approached Samuel.

"Sir, Major General Jackson has invited you to ride out to Plank Road with him," the aide told Samuel.

"Let me get my horse," Samuel replied. Samuel was happy to finally get away from the camp for some firsthand information.

The excitement he wanted came all too quickly. Major Jackson and his party were fired upon as he checked the picket lines.

Men were killed and wounded; confusion from all directions. Samuel jumped off his horse to see if he could help. The first man he came to had been killed. Gunfire continued. Samuel ducked and ran for more cover. The general's aide had motioned for him not to move.

"Mr. White, stay down. We need to get back to camp. Major General Jackson has been grievously wounded," the aide told him.

"What about the others with him?" Samuel asked.

"Hard to see right now, but we need to get back to camp."

Samuel didn't feel right leaving when he could help the wounded.

"I am going to stay and see if I can help anyone else that might be wounded," Samuel told the young aide.

"Then I will stay and help you. They have sent for an ambulance and the doctor for General Jackson."

Chapter 27

WILDERNESS. TAVERN

Night had fallen at the Wilderness Tavern. Mollie had come to where Ruby and the rest of the women were sitting around the fire. Sarah and Leona were fortunate and had found plants they would need to treat the wounded, to replenish their dwindling supplies.

"Ladies, I have brought a few things to give you with instructions on what we do with them," Mollie began. "Each one of you will be given a lantern with candles and a bell, and you will be allowed to enter the hospital and obtain bandages. We are allowed on the battlefields to check for the injured after the call to cease fire has been given by both sides. The bells are to let both sides know that there are nurses on the field. This agreement was made and has been honored by both armies. Most nights we will be able to go out, but tonight I do not think we will be able to go. There is gunfire everywhere, and I don't believe it is safe for anyone."

"What about the men inside and outside the hospital?" Sarah asked.

"We do what we can to help those outside, but we are not allowed inside to treat. Surgery takes place inside," Mollie replied.

"What about these doctors, Mollie?" Ruby asked. "What will they think about us helping where they cannot? What happens when we heal and save lives with nature and not their medicine?"

"There are so many men injured, you will probably not be noticed. Just stay away from the surgery and say nothing. We can do more out here to make a difference," Mollie told them.

Before Mollie could start another sentence, an ambulance with what appeared to be someone of importance arrived at the Wilderness Tavern.

Men ran to help carry the man into the hospital. Mollie got up and ran to see who had been brought to the camp. She returned a few moments later. Her head hung, shaking from side to side.

"Can we help?" Sarah stood.

"Not at this moment and I doubt they will allow any of us to get close to him," Mollie responded.

"Who the hell is it? General Lee himself?" Maud asked.

"Not General Lee, but someone almost as important. It's Major General Jackson. His own men shot him by accident," Mollie told them.

⤳

Sarah, Maud, and Ruby set up times to work and rest so that they did not exhaust themselves. Leona worked with Sarah, and the twins were split between Ruby and Maud.

Sarah walked away from the rest and maneuvered herself close to a window at the Tavern. She wanted to see and hear what was being done for Major General Jackson. She listened in the shadows as doctors talked about his shattered arm and their plans to amputate. Sarah worried but knew there would be nothing she or anyone else could do; no one would be interested in what a group of nurses had to say to help this man. She was about to turn and go back to where they had settled when a rider came fast and hard to the hospital with an injured soldier. The man, a civilian, had been kept from entering the building. Sarah could hear him arguing and continuing to push his way inside demanding someone look at the injuries to the young man he held in his arms. The doctors refused to help the injured aide due to the importance of General Jackson.

Sarah called to her friends to come. "Leona, bring me my bag. Ruby, Maud, have the twins make a pallet. We have work that needs to been done." Sarah turned back to the man.

"Sir, if you will bring him out here, I believe we'll be able to help."

Sarah tried to calm the man, but he did not respond to her request to come outside.

"Please anyone, someone, please help this boy," the man pleaded.

"Over here, young man. Quickly!" Ruby Belle's voice was louder than Sarah's, and it finally made him react.

He brought the young man outside to the pallet the women had rapidly prepared.

He laid down the wounded soldier and watched, silently.

In the glow of the fire and lanterns, Ruby looked up and smiled. "I think he will be just fine. Seems it went through his side, but we will check him over good. I will come and get you if we can't fix it."

"What happened?" Sarah asked.

"We were looking for more wounded after General Jackson was shot. We were trying to be careful and keep cover, but he was hit by what appeared to be crossfire. I didn't know where to go, so I followed the ambulance," the man rattled off to this woman.

"What is your name?" Sarah asked.

"My name is Samuel White. I am—"

"You are a reporter for the Franklin Weekly out of New York and my trusted friend for over six years." She couldn't believe the man she had wanted to meet and see for so many years had now appeared. His physical appearance impressed Sarah. He appeared to be in good health, and although he did not work on a farm field, he was muscular. His hair reminded her of James, but his eyes, even in the darkness of the night, shone like the sun. She should not be thinking of anything but his health, but Sarah couldn't stop looking at his eyes.

"You are the man writing about nurses. I am Sarah Bowen, and it is nice to meet you finally."

◯

Samuel sat down and tried to accept all that had happened to him in just the last few hours. He couldn't believe that the young girl, who helped him so many years ago when his mother died, stood before him now. He watched as these women took charge and cared for the injured aide. He should have been writing all that was going on, but he had become mesmerized by how quickly and efficiently they worked together.

"Are you hurt, Samuel?" Sarah walked over to check on him. "You have blood on your shirt. Are you injured?"

"I cannot believe you are here," he answered. "I cannot believe you're standing here in front of me. And no, it's not my blood. It's his." Samuel pointed to the aide.

"Let me look anyway, just to be sure," she told him.

"No, really. I am fine."

"Samuel, please do not argue with the nurse. It will only take a minute." She smiled.

Samuel finally took a moment to look, really look, at the woman who was kneeling and checking him for injuries. He had still thought of her as a child and not the woman before him.

He admired Sarah's lovely light-colored hair. He couldn't tell the color of her eyes, but he intended to look when the sun came up in the morning. He noticed a scent on her— lilac, very faint, but definitely lilac.

Sarah found two small cuts, which, if left untreated, could end up making him sick. She cleaned the cuts with water and then used witch hazel. A small bandage with a Calendula cream was placed over the wounds.

"Sarah, can you come look at this?" Maud called her to the young aide.

Sarah and Samuel both rose, and she increased her step, worrying that something had gone wrong.

Sarah kneeled to check on the young soldier and then looked to her friends, who stood around waiting for an answer.

"Samuel, the soldier you brought to the Wilderness Tavern is a woman."

∾

Sarah looked up at Samuel, who stared at her.

"Samuel, this will be an important story you will need to document but not publish until the war's end. I am going to ask you not to report this to her commanding officer," Sarah told him.

Samuel looked at the aide that had stood next to him during the battle that wounded Jackson. "Sarah, this woman never flinched, never faltered when we were pinned down. I never heard her cry out when she was shot. She just grabbed my arm and pointed to the blood. The stories I have heard are true. There are women fighting side by side with men on the battlefields," Samuel said. "Why should I be expected to keep this a secret? The nation should know about this."

"If we keep their secret, others that may be injured or sick will seek us out for help." Sarah stood and faced her friends. "It will be our job to heal these women and keep silent. Who are we to say their sacrifice was any less important than ours?"

"I see nothing here but a wounded soldier that needs to be cared for and sent back to his assignment," Leona said.

"I'll get him something for the pain," Maud told Sarah.

"Sadie, Sallie, let's get this man some food and clean clothes," Ruby told the twins.

Sarah leaned down and whispered into Ruby's ear, "I need you to bring my special blend of tea for sleep."

Ruby nodded her head.

"Sarah, how can you and these women promise to keep silent? That woman was almost killed and if sent back will probably go into battle," Samuel said.

"Samuel, do you not understand this is a choice? Her choice to fight, our choice to heal far from home. Think about your choices, past and present."

Sarah stared at him, thinking of all the letters they had exchanged over the years. She had never asked for a photo. Sarah regretted that now, looking at this handsome man.

"Your request goes against everything I have been taught as a reporter. How can you expect me to hold a story I can prove? As a man, I have been instructed since childhood to protect and respect women, I should report her."

"If you keep this story away from your readers for now, in time you will have more to add. One woman will be understood as just an occurrence—nothing else, but if you wait and gather more stories of women on the battlefields, you'll be able to substantiate that women were a fighting force during the war," Sarah explains.

"You make a good case," Samuel said, smiling at Sarah. "How long will you be in this area?"

"We will be here until this battle is over and do what we can for those left after the fighting stops. There are, as you can see, many who need our help. I will show you what we do and give you a story that will help all women who want to care for and heal the sick. We make a difference. We are able to take care of the severely injured and dying. We will show you how it is possible to heal with nature."

Ruby walked up with two cups of tea. Sarah took them and handed one to Samuel. "Samuel, will you wait to write this story?" Sarah asked him.

Samuel took the tea Sarah offered him and sat down next to a fallen tree.

"I'll hold the story for now, stay here, and observe. The cost will be information about your friendship with the Night Walker. I believe his name is Mack."

"I'm not sure what you are talking about," Sarah lied and walked over to get a quilt from supplies they had taken out of the wagon. She might have known this man for years through letters, but he had not yet gained her trust. Sarah knew his job would be to get a story, and Mack couldn't be spread across the pages for all to read. A story could lead to her imprisonment or death.

"Of course you do, Sarah. Edith told me about how close you two were at the healing house. You must be aware of the name this young man is making for himself. You seem to be the only one who knows anything about this spy who comes and goes at will," Samuel slurred slowly.

"Samuel, I admit I have met this Mack..." Sarah's words trailed off as Samuel slid to the ground. Sarah smiled and covered him with a quilt.

∽

"Well, that was easy," Maud told Sarah. "I was watching you lie to him about your friend."

"I have to know what information he has on Mack."

Sarah walked over to his horse and went through his belongings until she found his papers in the same pouch Mack had brought to the healing house. She walked back to the fire.

"I cannot have him writing about Mack. It will put him in danger, and that is something I will not allow," Sarah told Maud.

"And he can't report that injured aide either." Maud responded.

"Sadie and I are going out to check for injured men...and now women. Mollie got word it's safe for the nurses to look for the wounded. We need to use these bells and see how they are going to work for our safety," Ruby told them.

"Mom, you and Sadie take care out on the battlefields," Sallie said.

"We will go out after they come back, Sallie."

Maud wrapped her arm around Sallie's shoulders. Sarah was still going through the pouch.

"Sarah, don't you feel bad about putting him to sleep?" Leona laughed.

"No, should I?" Sarah started laughing, too. "He does have a nice smile, don't you think?"

"We didn't notice." Sallie began laughing, too.

"There. I found them," Sarah said.

She read through his notes to see what information Samuel had collected on the Night Walker. Sarah was pleased he knew only a name and nothing more about her friend. Sarah could now give him misinformation and know he couldn't call her on the lies she planned to tell him. Sarah put all his notes back and replaced the pouch. She walked over to the aide who had been shot and checked the wound. Sarah sat with her.

She had so many questions to ask. The aide began to wake up. Her eyes flooded with panic when she saw Sarah, realizing that she had been taken to the hospital.

"You and your secret are safe," Sarah told her.

"Thank you. I want to go back to my position. I am to be promoted and given more responsibility," the soldier said.

Sarah talked with the aide, never asking a name so that she would never be forced to identify this woman.

"You're not the only woman fighting in this war, are you?" Sarah asked.

"No, ma'am. There are others. How many, I do not know, but I am not alone."

"When you return to duty, and you will return, any female that is injured, sick, or needs medical attention of any kind will be welcomed here without fear of exposure."

The aide nodded her head and went back to sleep.

Her injuries were not life-threatening. Sarah walked to the main building and listened from a window where she heard that

Major General Jackson would be moved from the Wilderness Tavern and sent away to recover from his injuries. The arm that was amputated was taken and would be given a Christian burial, unlike those limbs that had been stacked behind the hospital to feed the flies.

It was just before daybreak when Dr. Buford Donaldson walked out to where the women had been treating and caring for the injured and sick.

"Young lady, I understand General Jackson's aide was brought out here, shot this past night," the doctor told Sarah.

"Yes, sir, he was," Sarah said cautiously.

"I assume he died from his injuries, since we were not able to treat him. Our immediate attention had to be given to General Jackson." The man shook his head.

"No, sir. He did not die."

"How is that possible? No one could have saved that young man. There is no one skilled enough out here to save anyone. Where is he? I want to see this aide who survived without a doctor's care," he screamed at Sarah.

Sarah had been taken by surprise and couldn't take him to where the aide was located for fear of exposing her gender.

"Dr. Donaldson, I have seen the young man you are inquiring about." Another physician walked up to the conversation.

"You have seen this injured aide, Dr. Bell?"

"Yes, I have. He was doing well and will be returning to duty in a few days."

"Good. I will return to the surgery. I knew it would not be possible for him to survive without true medical care from qualified personnel."

As the man walked off, Dr. Bell looked at Sarah.

"I have never liked that man since the first day I met him. I should introduce myself," he told Sarah. "My name is Dr.

Theodore Bell, at your service, friend to Mollie, the nurses, and all the women that have come to help here in this madness."

"I am Sarah Bowen, and I can tell you that the people of Greenville miss you."

"You must have met Edith Blake."

"Yes, she is now in charge of a healing house south of Greenville, helping those who are in need," Sarah proudly told him.

"South of Greenville? That house was the home of a wonderful woman, a healer and a good friend. The whole family died, murdered." Doc Bell looked at the ground as he responded.

Sarah wanted to ask more questions but felt this would be all the information he would reveal.

"I know who you are and what you and your ladies are doing to help these poor souls. I can help keep the other physicians from interfering with your work as long as you stay away from the main building. I am the only one who will come out and check these men. I try and keep them clean, and those with other illnesses are separated. I believe in the use of nature to heal, and you are welcome to use it here freely."

"Thank you. We will do all that we can to help."

"I am afraid you will be called upon to give more in the days ahead," he said. "I am glad to see you and the other ladies. You will receive no reprimand from me, only my undying thanks for all you do for these men. If you'll excuse me, I have not slept. I am going to find a bed before the fighting begins again."

Sarah watched Doc Bell weave his way through the living and dead then disappear into the Wilderness Tavern.

∽

Samuel woke to the smell of coffee and gunpowder. He tried to remember when he had lain down by this tree and covered himself with a quilt.

"Good morning, Mr. White," Ruby Belle said, looking down at him. "Slept well, did you?" She laughed and walked away.

"Yes, I did thank you," he responded.

Leona walked by, laughing. "Would you like some coffee, Mr. White?"

"Yes, please. Where is Sarah?"

"Asleep," Maud told him as she walked by. "She was up all night while we slept. She checked on the more severely wounded—several died."

Samuel got up from the folds of the quilt and took a cup of coffee from Leona. The fighting had begun at first light. These women had worked off and on all night, resting when they could find a moment. This morning they looked fresh and had a smile, despite knowing that it would be another day facing wounded and dying men. He went to his horse, took his pouch, and went back to find a place to write. Samuel had so much to report since leaving the Allen's' in Gaston. He had felt exhilarated during the fight and didn't understand why he fell asleep. Samuel began with his series and wrote all that had happened to Emma. Emma's story would give another face to the war.

He continued to write as the war went on around him: the story of Major General Jackson and Samuel's part in the story with the injured aide. He was anxious to talk with these women who had traveled away from their homes, families, and friends to give of themselves in this bloody field of bodies. Samuel hoped to obtain several stories about women fighting side by side with men on the battlefield. He knew there would be stories of women injured and dying that must be documented. Samuel would honor Sarah's request to remain silent for now. His major project would be identifying the Night Walker and telling his story. Time had slipped away. Samuel stood to stretch and turned to look for another cup of coffee when he saw Sarah walking toward him. She was lovelier than he first thought. How could he have not made a trip to Georgia to meet this woman? Someone who has always been there to support him.

He took in the smallest details: the blue dress she wore matched her eyes, and there were small pink flowers inside the tiny checked pattern of her dress.

He watched Sarah pulled a loose strand of blonde hair back into the bun at the nape of her neck as she walked toward the smell of coffee. Samuel knew it had been a long night, and she could use a cup of something hot. When Sarah arrived to where he stood, Samuel didn't hear the words she spoke, but looked at the pink heart around her neck. Then he noticed a scent, the same scent he had smelled last night. Lilacs—she smells like lilacs.

"Samuel, did you hear me? I asked if you slept well last night." Sarah smiled and tried not to laugh. She then looked into his eyes that were so green they seemed to see into the depth of her soul.

"Yes, yes, I did. Thank you. What type of stone is in your necklace?" Samuel asked. He then reached out, picked the pendant up from her chest, and then gently returned it.

Sarah's face became flushed. She excused herself to get a cup of coffee and returned, sitting down on a tree stump. Samuel walked over and kneeled down close to her.

"This stone is called rose quartz," Sarah told him.

Samuel listened as she explained the importance of the pendant and about the love her parents had for each other.

"It is said that rose quartz will bring a true love to you."

"Has it?" he asked.

"Not yet. But there is always another day ahead of me." Sarah reached to check the cuts she had treated the night before. "They're beginning to heal."

∽

"What are you two doing?" Leona asked.

"Watching love set in the hearts of two people, girl," Maud told her.

"Yep, I am afraid you're right, my Texas friend," Ruby laughed. "Girls, we need to get busy. Leona, you and the twins go see if you can find more of what you and Sarah found yesterday in the woods. I have several pots of fresh water boiling."

"I will take some men and go see if I can find water that isn't ruined," Maud said.

"Ms. Ruby, my cycle has come again, and it is more than last month. Do you think you could help me find some heavy rags?" Leona was embarrassed.

"Don't you worry, girl. We'll fix you up good," Ruby whispered to her. "It's time to go to work, ladies. We have another long day ahead of us and souls to save if the Lord wills. Mollie Mae, don't you run off, woman. We need to talk a few minutes. Where do you keep extra pots? We have broths to make and teas to brew. Where did you say we could get clean bandages? Not those nasty things you brought us last night. We had to burn them." Ruby chased after Mollie.

Everyone scurried around getting ready for more wounded.

⌒

Sarah looked up as the others began their work. "I need to get busy and help the others, Samuel."

Samuel reached and took her hand. "I will be here, and you owe me an interview. We have a lot to discuss."

"If you want a story, all you have to do is stand around here for a few hours. You will not have enough paper or pencils to write about all you see. I'll talk to you later in the day if there is time. Just look for me. I will be here." Sarah joined the others to start another day of helping and healing.

Chapter 28

FRANKLIN WEEKLY
TWO WEEKS AFTER THE BATTLE
AT CHANCELLORSVILLE

"Joseph, what do you mean you can't find him?" Franklin screamed.

"He wasn't where we had arranged to meet at Chancellorsville. I searched everywhere, talked to all the officers, other reporters, and no one had seen or heard of him since the battle at Washington. The loss of Union forces at Chancellorsville had the armies scattered. The wounded and dying were everywhere. I thought he might have come back here to bring his stories or to see you and his family before traveling to the next battle," Joseph said, trying to calm his boss.

"Well, he hasn't come home." Franklin sat back down. "Joseph, I want you to go back to Chancellorsville, but this time, check where the Confederates are located. You have your papers, right?"

"Yes, sir. Right here." He patted his breast pocket.

"I want you to think very carefully about your position here. Don't even think of coming back into my office without laying eyes on Samuel or bringing him back to New York. Do I make myself clear?"

"Perfectly," Joseph said, and he ran out the door.

Franklin sat down, leaned back, and reached for his bottom desk drawer.

Samuel, what have you gotten yourself into this time?

Chapter 29

CHANCELLORSVILLE

The last few weeks had been enlightening, frustrating, and unbelievable. Samuel had enough information to write volumes about the nurses, doctors, and the devastation of this war. Sarah and the others had taken him to their hearts. They had shown the uses of all that surrounded them in nature. He had watched these women heal with plants and flowers. The cuts Samuel had were healed, leaving almost no scars. Many of the plants and herbs they used grew in Julia's garden back home. He had made note of the book Sarah carried along with her mother's personal diary of plants. Samuel had interviewed Confederate soldiers and officers, and watched as dozens of women dressed as men, some with rank as high as captain, came to seek medical help. Many of these women had old injuries, which were never treated due to their worry of being discovered and dismissed from service.

It was now the beginning of June. The days were long and warm. Samuel had let Sarah put him off long enough about the Night Walker. She had promised to tell him this evening what she knew. He looked forward to obtaining information about Mack; however, what he wanted most he had not been able to obtain: time alone with Sarah. He had been a fool to not see what this woman truly was all the years they had been writing to one another. Grief and anger were strange friends and could blind a man to what should be important: family and friends. Samuel did know that Sarah had strong convictions, many of which did not coincide with Southern beliefs.

"Samuel, I am sorry to bother you, but we have been told there are troops heading to Middleburg. We will be leaving soon," Sarah said.

Samuel could detect her relief in avoiding the conversation about Mack.

"Not a problem. I'll go with you. I can write as I go," Samuel said.

"Samuel! Samuel White!" a voice called from a distance.

"Joseph, what are you doing here?"

"I am trying to keep my job and my life. Franklin was mad, upset, and worried as hell when you didn't meet me at the assigned place."

Sarah slipped away as their conversation continued.

"Sarah, don't go." Samuel ran to grab her hands.

"I'm not going anywhere except to start preparing for the next battle: find scarce supplies, food, and water that isn't tainted," she told him.

"This will not take long. I just need to get my stories and send them back with Joseph. Don't forget you owe me a story about Mack."

"I know, I know. Tonight we will talk." Sarah squeezed his hands and walked off.

"Samuel, what are you doing here?" Joseph asked. "This isn't the story you should be writing about. There isn't anything here worth reporting."

"Joseph, that's where you are wrong. There is a story here that affects all of us, and one I am becoming personally involved in."

"I've kept my promise and laid eyes on you. I would appreciate a letter to the boss along with the stories that are ready to go."

"Tell Franklin that these stories are going to be some of the hardest he will ever have to print." Samuel quickly wrote Franklin a note asking him to tell his father and Julia that he was well and traveling with Confederate nurses.

"Good afternoon. Can we do anything for you today?" Maud asked.

"Maud, this is Joseph Bines. He works at the Franklin Weekly and is here to get my stories. He is about to leave."

"Not before we give you a bite to eat and some strong coffee. Samuel, where are your manners? Come with me, Joseph, and I will show you how we Texans feed a hungry man," Maud said.

Joseph looked at Samuel for approval. Samuel nodded.

"Thank you, Miss—?" Joseph said, unsure.

"It's Maud, honey. You can just call me Maud." She took his arm, practically dragging him to where the food was cooking.

Samuel laughed. *I hope he survives.*

⌒

Samuel gathered his stories for Joseph to take back to New York. He headed out to find Maud and Joseph. The sound of a woman screaming and horses galloping off with a wagon sent Samuel running after everyone in the camp. He saw Maud on the ground.

"Maud, are you hurt?" Samuel asked.

Maud moved to reveal Joseph lying on the ground, bleeding and moaning in pain.

Leona was the next to arrive. Maud told her, "Go find Sarah, now!"

"What can I do to help?" Samuel asked.

"He needs to stay still and not move. Samuel, I need you to hold this on his head to help stop the bleeding." Maud handed Samuel a piece of her dress and looked down at Joseph. "You hang in there, honey. Sarah will fix you up."

Sarah and Doc Bell both came running to where Joseph was lying.

"Don't move him," Doc Bell told everyone. Joseph had a broken arm and a bad cut across his forehead. "Sarah, do you have any comfrey?"

"Yes, I do."

"I figured you would," he said, smiling. "I need you to get it. I will need your help."

Samuel's concern for his friend tensed every muscle in his body; his face was strained with worry.

"Samuel, come with me. We have things to go get to help your friend." Sarah took his hand. "Samuel, now!"

He followed her like a child. Samuel and Sarah returned with the supplies Doc Bell requested.

"Son, you are in the best hands possible," Doc Bell explained to Joseph. The doctor splinted   Joseph's arm after Sarah used comfrey on the break.

Maud made a tea from calendula and chamomile to soothe him, and used a cream made from calendula to treat his cut. She saved the moonshine for later. Samuel helped move Joseph as gently as possible to a pallet.

"I'll stay with him," Maud said."It was my fault he got hurt. He offered to help get a water barrel out of the wagon for me. The next thing I knew, the horses bolted, and he was on the ground hurt."

Sarah took Samuel's hand, and they walked away from where Joseph was lying.

"Samuel, it will be at least a week before he can travel any great distance. Is there anyone else who can take your stories back, or can you find another courier?"

"There isn't anyone I trust with my stories." Samuel looked toward Joseph."I am going to have to leave and take these stories back. They are too important and need to be put into print."

"I guess our conversation about Mack will have to wait until the next time I see you." Sarah was asking more than telling.

"Oh, you're not going to get off that easy. I will leave at first light tomorrow. I'll expect to see you at dark for our interview."

"Then I'll see you at dark." Sarah smiled and walked away to check on Joseph and the other wounded and then back to packing and obtaining supplies.

∾

Mack had found her way to the Wilderness Tavern. Over the last two days and nights, she had hidden, and watched all that had been going on in the camp. She couldn't believe Sarah would tell that reporter anything about her or what she did for the South. Mack had a plan to talk with Sarah before the interview began tonight. She hoped Sarah would continue to be the true friend she had always known her to be. She couldn't let this man know her true identity and the purpose of the Night Walker.

∾

Samuel made arrangements to leave tomorrow at first light to go back to New York. He would have to ride long hours to get to the Weekly and back to Sarah. He had watched her work all day. This woman was truly unbelievable: healing, cleaning, packing, cooking, and then she went out into the woods to find plants. Ruby and the twins found help filling the water barrels. Maud continued to baby Joseph. Sarah made everyone in the camp boil the water. He didn't understand the reasoning but intended to ask her one day. She kept clean as much as possible in the heat. Men were washed; bandages were kept clean and changed. Many of the men that these women had cared for would live to see another day.

∾

Sarah felt the length of the day, but she would keep her promise and talk with Samuel. She wished they could forgo the conversation about Mack, but she would give him all the misinformation he wanted. She had found a few moments to take care of personal needs and find something to eat. The movement behind her forced Sarah to turn and see Mack's familiar face in a stand of trees. She grabbed a basket as though she was going to gather herbs. Sarah headed to the trees to see her friend. She looked to the place Mack had appeared, but she was now gone.

That girl can disappear faster than smoke on a windy day.

"Mack. Mack, where are you?" Sarah whispered.

"Sarah, I am here." The voice came from behind her. Sarah turned and they hugged each other. "What's wrong?" Sarah asked.

"That's the reporter from North Carolina, isn't it?" Mack asked.

"Yes, he is. Why? How long have you been here, Mack?"

"Two days and nights."

Sarah knew that Mack had been around the camp listening to conversations and was worried about Samuel.

"Well, the only thing you have to worry about is all the lies I am about to tell him. I would never take any chance on your safety. You know that," Sarah told her. "Mack, this is a man I have been corresponding with for six years."

"What? How is it that you know this man that is so very far away from Georgia?" Mack's language was perfect.

"Goodness, you have been practicing, young lady. I am impressed." Sarah smiled.

"I knew there must be a connection somewhere between the two of you. He looks at you the way I want James to look at me."

Sarah blushed. "I have not shared my feelings with anyone since Mother died. Since the day Samuel arrived in camp, our childhood friendship has grown into something deeper, at least for me."

Mack smiled. "Do you mind if I listen tonight?"

"Mack, that is your decision, as long as you don't laugh and fall out of a tree into his lap. That would be a little difficult to explain," Sarah quipped. "Do you need any food or water?"

"I helped myself early this morning. I didn't think you would mind." Mack laughed and disappeared into the depth of the trees.

How does she do that?

When Sarah cleared the trees, Samuel could be seen talking to Leona and Ruby, who were both laughing. He really does have a wonderful smile. Sarah laid her hand to her heart, touching the rose quartz necklace.

Day had now turned to night and the time for the conversation. Sarah and Samuel found a quiet place to talk alone. The twins brought some dinner and coffee and then ran off giggling.

"What was that about?" Samuel asked.

"You tell me."

They both picked at their food, and finally Samuel started.

"I know you and this Mack are friends. He is becoming as famous as the Gray Ghost. What can you tell me about him?"

Sarah knew that Mack would be close enough to hear their conversation.

"Samuel, you have to understand I can only tell you the limited knowledge I have on this very brave young man," Sarah said, beginning the lie that lasted for almost two hours.

Samuel wrote and made notes, impressed with all the information Sarah had about the Night Walker. He felt he had enough to begin his special report on this spy. The glow of the fire made Sarah look angelic.

"Sarah, tell me about your brothers. What do you want to do after the war?"

Sarah told Samuel things about her brothers and her home she had never revealed in her letters to him over the years. There were personal details of the love and worry she had for Ethan, being in Texas, so far away from home, as well as the hope she had that James understood her need to leave and that the farm continued to prosper in her absence.

"I want to return home and teach others the art of healing with nature," Sarah said. "What about you, Samuel? Do you have special plans after this war is over?"

Samuel realized he had never thought about his own life or future beyond the present day. He poured out his soul to Sarah without hesitation. He had never known any woman that was interested in anything but his money. Sarah had never mentioned money in all the years he had known her. She truly cared about people and how to ease their suffering.

"Your family and your friend Franklin sound wonderful. You are very lucky, you know that?"

"Yes, I know. I just didn't realize it until now," Samuel told her. "Thank you."

"For what?"

"For reminding me how important my family and friends are to me."

"You're welcome." Sarah smiled. "I need to go rest and so do you. There isn't much time before you have to leave."

"I want to see you before I leave. Will you be awake?"

"I will try." Sarah walked off to where she had a pallet made for sleep.

Samuel took his notes and put them in his pouch. He took the quilt that had been issued to him and tried to rest, but the trip back home weighed heavily on his mind. He didn't want to go when what he had come to care about was here.

Samuel didn't really sleep, and as the blackness of the night turned into the lavender and blues of the morning, he rose and saddled his horse.

Mollie and Ruby were up making coffee and beginning breakfast.

"Samuel, don't you worry about your friend Joseph," Mollie told him.

Ruby patted Samuel on the back and told him, "Mollie will take good care of him after we are gone and make sure he gets back to New York safely."

Samuel looked around the camp for Sarah. "I can't thank you enough for watching after him." He finally saw Sarah walking toward him with supplies. He wanted to take her back to New York, this very moment, away from all the death and disease that surrounded her.

"I thought you might need a few things." Sarah handed him the small sack of supplies she had gathered for him.

Samuel took the sack, put it on his horse, and turned back to the smell of lilacs. He started to speak but instead took Sarah into his arms and kissed her softly, gently. When their lips were no longer touching, he whispered in her ear, "Look for me, Sarah. I will be back."

Before Sarah could say anything, he was on his horse and gone.

She touched her lips and turned to face her friends, who were all smiling.

"Do you think James will ever kiss me like that?" Mack asked Sarah. Mack had walked out of the trees and up to her friend, who hadn't even heard her approach.

"I don't know, Mack."

"Sarah, we need to get busy and finish packing. Middleburg is only about three to four days from here, but we need to go," Ruby told her.

"I know. Mack, can you stay for a while?" Sarah asked, hoping she would, even if only for a few hours.

"Just for the day, Sarah. I have work to do. There is something big about to happen, and we will all be a part of it."

"Then let's enjoy the time we have today."

Chapter 30

MIDDLEBURG, VIRGINIA
JUNE 19, 1863

Sarah searched for more bandages as the wounded continued to come. She and the other women walked the battlefield looking for the injured soldiers left there after dark. Mollie was correct about the armies honoring the sound of the bells after the fighting had ended for the day. Sarah had heard the bells, seen the lights from the Northern nurses, and heard the calls of their men crying for help. Water continued to be scarce, along with supplies. Sarah had seen a house about a mile back when they arrived three or four days ago, just before the battle began. She was sure it was empty. She would take Leona and go search for anything that was useable. Sarah hoped there might be a garden and vegetables. They would look for anything green to cook that would have sustenance for them and the men they were treating.

Ruby and Maud made candles; the twins made soap, using instructions and the sunflower oil Sarah gave them. The lye had been too harsh for the wounds they were seeing, and the recipe she used had belonged to her mother. She only wished there were oats or mint available to add.

"Sarah, we need you over here," Leona called.

"I am on my way." Sarah grabbed the dwindling supply of creams. She hesitated and hoped that Samuel had made it back to New York safely. He should have been there by now.

"Sarah," Leona called again.

Sarah stopped thinking of Samuel and went to help.

Chapter 31

NEW YORK
JUNE 19

Samuel, why are you in such a hurry? You have only been home a couple of days," Franklin said.

"I need to go. I stopped in a couple of Union camps for information on the way here. There is a huge buildup of troops and skirmishes. They all seem to be going toward a place called Gettysburg."

"Are you sure that's the only reason you are in such a hurry to leave? I have read your interviews with Sarah Bowen. Your writing style is different with this woman—softer, a more caring attitude. A style I have not seen from you until now."

"It shows, doesn't it?" Samuel looked at Franklin. "She is not like any woman I have ever met before. Her beliefs and the way she heals...I have never seen her ask for anything in return, not even an extra hour to rest. I need to get back. I have to find her."

Franklin knew there was nothing he could say to sway Samuel. "What can I do to help with your stories?" he asks.

"I have all my stories on "The Women Who Travel in War" up-to-date. These are going to be the most important part of the war besides its end and where we go to heal our country. I will finish them when I find Sarah and bring her home."

"Take care of yourself. I can't wait to meet this woman that has become such a part of your soul," Franklin said. "Do you have time for a drink?"

"Absolutely. I always have time for that, my friend."

Samuel took a breath and watched as Franklin poured them both a glass.

"I am leaving in the morning. Have you had any word from Joseph?"

"I received a cable from him. He will be back here in a few days, thanks to the good care he has received from someone called Maud."

"I have already said my good-byes at home, so if it's all right with you, I want to sleep here so I can get an early start."

"Your old bed is made and the sheets are clean."

Samuel took a stack of papers and his notes, put them into a file, and handed it to Franklin.

"Can you put these in the safe until I get back?" Samuel handed Franklin the folder.

"What is this? Another story?"

"Yes, something that will make the Weekly famous. I would appreciate it if you would not read them until I can get back to finish the story. You know how I am about having all the information verified before it goes to print. This will be an important part to add to my book, a special ending."

Franklin laughed and placed the folder in his safe.

"You've piqued my curiosity, Samuel, but I will do what you ask."

"Good, I have one thing left to do before I leave." Samuel finished his drink quickly.

"Where to now?" Franklin asks.

"I have to get to the bank before father locks the door." He grabbed his coat and headed out the door.

Franklin wanted to open the safe and read the file Samuel gave him, but he would keep his promise and wait until Samuel returned home with his Sarah.

Chapter 32

Within A Few Miles of Ashby's Gap
June 19

Mack had been traveling for the last two days, searching for Long-
street and her contact. Skirmishes were everywhere, but she had
seen massive movements toward the small town of Gettysburg.
She had been sitting in a tree for a few hours while Grey rested
and fed on fresh grass they found safely away from the main road.
She remembered the last tree she had sat in, listening to Sarah
tell lies about her to tell Samuel. Mack had noticed movement
of a Confederate troop, and she had chosen to just let them go
by. She was about to doze off when she heard a familiar voice.

"Sergeant!" the lieutenant called. "Yes, sir."

"We can stop here for a few minutes and give the men a
short rest."

"Right away, lieutenant." The sergeant turned his mount
and gave the order to the men to stop and rest.

No, this isn't possible. She then saw the lieutenant dismount,
walk up, and lean on the tree she sat in. The lieutenant took off
his cap and ran a hand through his sweaty brown hair. Tears
welled up in Mack's eyes as she saw a long scar across the left
side of his face. He reached in his breast pocket and took out a
much worn red paper heart and held it.

"Lieutenant Bowen," a young soldier said as he approached James.

"Yes, Leonard."

"Major General Mc Laws sent word, sir. You are needed." James nodded his head, replaced his cap, and mounted his horse.

"Sergeant, I will be back shortly. Get the men up and moving. Leonard, you are with me.   Sergeant, a horse if you would for the private. Sorry, Leonard, I mean corporal," James said.

"Yes, sir," Leonard answered and ran to find a horse.

The Georgia 53rd moved out of the area.

Mack did something she hadn't since leaving the Bowen farm in February.

She cried.

Chapter 33

FOUR DAYS LATER AT MIDDLEBURG

"Ruby, I need to take the wagon and go search for food and supplies," Sarah argued with Ruby.

"It isn't safe, girl."

"Then give me your pistol, and I'll take Maud if you want. If we do not take the time to search for plants and replenish our medical supplies, we're going to be in serious trouble before the next battle."

"Leona," Ruby called out.

Leona came and joined the two women.

"Yes," Leona said timidly.

"Go get Maud and the wagon. Sarah, you take chances with your life," Ruby scolded her.

"If I don't, others could die."

Ruby got her guns and gave them to her friends.

Leona had found a couple of soldiers to load several small empty water containers into the wagon. If they found clean water, they would not be able to lift a full barrel. Leona put a couple of lanterns and their bells in the wagon. They would need them when day turned to night and they returned to camp.

Sarah, Maud, and Leona took the wagon and left the camp.

"Sarah, how far is this place you saw?" Maud asked.

"If I am right, it is about a mile or two from here," Sarah told them. "Leona, did I see you using extra bandages a few weeks ago?"

"Sarah, I had a really bad cycle and needed something thicker. I am sorry, but Ruby said it was fine."

"Sorry, I didn't know."

Sarah was right about the location of the house; it was only about a mile from where the hospital had been set up. The three pulled up to the front of the empty home.

"Leona, you and Maud go into the house and see if there is anything we can use as bandages. Also, look for coffee, flour, anything that hasn't been taken before we got here. Clothes see if there are any clothes and look for a cellar under the house."

Sarah was talking fast; giving direction so they would look for only the items needed and could leave before dark. She walked out to what appeared to be a garden. She had found carrots, onions, and a few beans. She searched for greens and found them. There was fresh mint. Sarah realized it was a huge herb garden. She turned to run back to the wagon when she heard her name being called.

"Miss Sarah. Miss Sarah, is that you?"

Sarah turned and saw Chloe, one of Uncle Mike's slaves.

"Chloe, what are you doing here? Where is your baby? Are you alone out here?"

"Miss Sarah, can yous come with me?" Chloe's voice was low.

"Just a minute. If I disappear, the others will come looking for me."

Sarah ran to the house. "Leona, Maud, I have found a large herb garden. I am going to start gathering what I can."

"I'll come help you," Leona told Sarah.

"No, Leona. I want you to stay with Maud. The two of you need to stay together. I will be just outside."

"Then take this, Sarah." Leona handed Sarah the pistol and a lantern.

Sarah took the gun, put it in her pocket, and then went back to where Chloe was hiding.

Chloe took Sarah deep into the trees to a small shack holding six runaway slaves looking for their guide to the Underground Railroad.

"This is Miss Sarah," Chloe said, introducing Sarah to the others. Baby Sarah was being held by one of the men. "Miss Sarah, this is Nace, Sarah's paw."

"Chloe said you saved her and my baby. I thanks you," Nace said.

"You are all in great danger here," Sarah told them.

"We gots nowhere else to go, Miss Sarah. Our guide ain't here to meet us. We have to waits."

"Do you have food and water?"

"Yes, ma'am. We took some from the garden before you gots here and there is a small spring a ways from this shack on the other side of the barn. Miss Sarah, can we trust you not tell about us?" Chloe asked.

"Chloe, is anyone hurt or in need of medical attention?" Sarah asked.

"No, ma'am. We is all good."

"Then God keep you and may your travels be safe. What has passed between us at this moment goes no further." Sarah took Chloe's hands and squeezed them. She started out the door when Chloe called after her. Sarah turned around.

"Mr. Mike did all that you asked him to do. I just wants my baby and us to be free."

"I know." Sarah smiled. She walked away from the shack and began to gather everything she could that could be harvested.

Sarah returned to the house. They had been fortunate to find sheets, clothes, and a food cellar. Leona found a few onions and potatoes that weren't rotten. The biggest prize was the dozens of jars of honey.

"Y'all look at this here," Maud called. "I believe this is some home brew."

"Take it," Sarah told her.

"Leona, there has to be a root cellar with flowers and plants," Sarah said.

"What about water?" Maud asked. "I found an empty barrel we can use.

"Back behind the house on the other side of the barn, there is a stream." Sarah carefully guided them away from the shack.

The women worked for hours, taking anything that could be used. They loaded fresh water, and Sarah found a small root cellar. There were carrier oils and containers of creams, some already made with herbs, others a base. Roots, dried flowers, herbs she didn't have time to identify now but would when they returned.

"Maud, when we get back, I need to find something to make a warming cupboard out of to dry some of these flowers and herbs," Sarah said.

"We can use one of the small tents, build a smoldering fire, and dry them," Leona interjected.

As the women left the house with a full wagon of supplies, Sarah looked back and hoped those in the shack found safe passage to a new life.

"What are you looking at, Sarah?" Leona asked.

"Nothing. I am just thinking about who lived in these homes we go through and hoping they will forgive us for taking without asking. There is so much to do when we get back and little time to do it in before we go."

"We will manage, Sarah," Maud said.

"Sarah, did you take one of the lanterns into the root cellar?" Leona asked.

"Are we missing one?"

"Yes," Leona responded.

"Then I guess I left it there. There was so much to gather, I just forgot it," Sarah lied.

∾

Chloe, Nace, baby Sarah, and the others slowly and quietly traveled along the route with their guide after dark.

"Do you trust her, Chloe?" Nace asked.

"With my soul, Nace, with my soul," Chloe told him.

"Do you think she forgot the lantern, Chloe?" the guide asked.

"No, Miss Sarah doesn't forget. She left it for us to help light the way."

Chapter 34

GETTYSBURG, PENNSYLVANIA
JULY 1

*The days were beginning to run together for Sarah since Chancel-*lorsville. They had been to Middleburg, Upperville, Hanover, and now they had arrived late afternoon in Gettysburg. The ladies were no longer naive to the horrors of war. Once they had settled in a safe place, all went out looking for plants, flowers, and any herbs that had not been destroyed. Trees cut down for shelter and fires, gardens trampled by horses, men, and wagons had left little for them to obtain in many of the towns they had traveled through. Each of them had gained knowledge quickly and took nothing for granted. The summer swelter had become unbearable; the remains of men and animals could be seen along the roadside, bloated, rotting, and forgotten except by the flies that feasted on them. Many times Maud had run off the curs feeding on bodies not buried quickly. The stench of the dead was ignored in order for them to do their job. They had all learned sadly to take from the dead that which would help the living—something that was becoming all too easy and familiar.

The women had taken a moment to stretch and take stock of their supplies.

"Sarah, we are needed at the Lutheran church where the Confederate doctors have set up a hospital," Ruby called out.

Guns and cannons fired all around them. None of the women ducked or flinched anymore.

"We're ready," Sarah told Ruby.

"Back in the wagon, girls," Ruby yelled to them.

When Sarah and the rest arrived at the church, they were happy to see a friend, Doc Bell. Everyone got out and gathered around him.

"Doc Bell, how long have you been here?" Ruby asked.

"Long enough to know I will need women like you inside to help me." He looked toward the church. "I will watch over and protect you as much as possible from the ignorance of the educated. I hope you have something in that wagon for pain and fever. We are low on everything except whiskey."

The women looked at the carnage that surrounded the church, inside and out.

"Sarah, what can we do? There are so many of them." Leona's voice was shaky.

"This is nothing we have not faced before. We will do what we have done in the past—we will assist, give comfort, and heal where it is possible," Sarah told them. "Sadie, you and Sallie unload and find a place for us to rest when we are not working."

"Find a tree to put the horses under," Ruby told them.

"Ruby, we need to go outside and set up an area for the men who are not severely wounded," Maud shouted. "We need to be able to get them patched up and back to the fight."

Sarah took Leona's hand. "Are you ready?" Sarah asked.

"I think so."

"Time to go to work, then," Sarah told her, sweat running off both their faces.

They walked into the sea of men crying, begging, and pleading for help.

Day turned into night, and the women took their lanterns and bells and headed to the battlefields looking for wounded that could be saved. Some returned with wounded, but many were lost. They returned to where the twins set up a campsite for them.

"Did anyone find any women?" Sarah asked her friends. Each night, they talked to one another about the injured and dying men and women they cared for on the battlefield. This seemed to help ease the burden they all carried.

"I found one," Sadie said. "And Sallie thought she found three. Their bodies were..."

Ruby went over to her daughters and put her arms around both of them. "We understand. You both did well out there tonight."

"Did anyone else find any women on the battlefield?" Sarah asked again. They all shook their heads. "I am proud of all of you. What we are doing is not easy for anyone. I have seen the burial details. Men are having trouble with the state of the bodies. We are not heartless. We have feeling and emotions, too."

"Y'all need to know how glad I am to know all of you," Maud began."I have something I need to tell all of you."

"You're not pregnant, are you?" Sallie asked. Sadie elbowed her sister.

"No, I ain't pregnant, and I ain't got no husband."

"Maud, why did you tell us you were married?" Sarah asked.

"Leaving Texas to come help wouldn't have looked proper if I hadn't had a purpose to go. I made up the story to tell folks when I left. Since I met all of you, I no longer need that lie to do what I feel deep inside, and that is to help others. Sarah, you and these ladies have changed and will change the way that women will be looked upon as healers and nurses. If what you tell us about that young man Samuel is true, his stories will encourage all women that have the calling to heal."

"Maud, is that the only reason? I saw you and Joseph just before he was sent back home to New York," Leona teased.

"We talked a bit. Maybe when this here war is done, something might work out." Maud smiled at everyone.

"We should try and sleep," Leona said.

"In this heat? Good luck," Sallie responded.

Sarah stood and walked away from the heat of the fire. She had tried not to think about Samuel, but hoped he had remained in New York. If he should return, she prayed he would stay away from the fighting until they could safely find one another.

She touched her necklace. I do not have a good feeling about this battle.

JULY 2

Mack followed the Georgia 53rd. She no longer had a job to do at this point. All information had been delivered. But Mack needed to be close to James even though she couldn't reveal herself at the moment. Longstreet's troops were close to Black Horse Tavern. There had been some confusion between officers, and she was unable to get close enough to hear all the conversation.

"Lieutenant Bowen, what's going on?" Leonard asked.

"Corporal, I am not sure. We may be turning around and heading in a different direction. We are too exposed here," James told him. "Leonard, stay close when the battle begins. I can't afford to train another corporal."

"Yes, sir. I will be like a fly in honey."

∼

Samuel arrived in Gettysburg thirty minutes before one of the fiercest battles of the war began. He had located several reporters and quickly made an assessment of where Union and Confederate troops were located. He knew that Sarah and the women with her would be where they were of best use to the wounded. His next question to his fellow reporters was "Where are the Confederate hospitals?"

JULY 3

Ruby stood in the doorway of the church with her lantern, bell, and medical pouch, waiting for the others. She watched as everyone collected their supplies in the homemade pouches and smiled at the individuality of each one. Maud had made hers from saddlebags, Leona and the twins used empty flour sacks, and Sarah took what once belonged to her mother.

"Sarah, we need to go while the fighting has stopped. There may not be a lot of time before they start up again," Ruby told her.

"Ruby, where do you get all your information?" Maud asked as she threw the saddlebags over her shoulder.

"It's a secret. Can't tell you," Ruby said, smiling at Maud.

"Does it have anything to do with where you took that small bottle of moonshine a few hours ago?" Leona laughs.

"Could be girl, could be."

Sarah finished bandaging another amputated limb. She had covered the poorly done surgical site with honey and clean bandages. Whiskey seemed to be the only thing she had to give for the pain. Sarah knew that Ruby had been trading moonshine for information with soldiers from the field. They'd tell her where there were injured men needing help. Sarah picked up her pouch and walked over to where Ruby and the others were gathered.

"Ruby, we have to find something else besides whiskey to give these men for pain. I need to go find plants and flowers. There has to be something out here that hasn't been destroyed. The whiskey we are using for their pain is making the bleeding hard to control," Sarah told her.

"I sent Sallie, Sadie, and Leona out earlier," Ruby said.

Sarah looked up in horror.

"I sent one of the ambulance drivers with them and a soldier. They were lucky and found vegetable gardens and flowers, and Leona brought a large amount of tansy back with her. There was a large donation of clean sheets made to us."

"What about water?" Sarah asked.

"Not as easy to come by as we would like," Maud said walking up with her lantern. "I ain't used to this heaviness in the air."

The walk was long and difficult. Fires, smoke, and the screaming of men, boys, and probably women awaited them. Their dress hems became saturated in the puddles of blood they walked through but couldn't see. Only the added heaviness made them aware they had arrived at their destination.

They all stood and bowed their heads as Ruby began the blessing for tonight's work.

"God help us and those we are here to attend. Protect all who walk this field to heal. Amen."

"Amen," they all said together.

The ringing of bells began.

∽

Mack searched the area of the wheat field and the peach orchard where the heaviest fighting and loss of life from both sides had occurred. She had only one thought at this moment. I have to find James alive. God, please.

Mack walked through bloody fields turning body after body over, looking at their faces. There were so many that had been disfigured or had no face at all. She couldn't be sure. When there was not a recognizable face, she checked their breast pockets for the red heart she'd made; it seemed a lifetime ago. Mack worried he might be wounded. She reached for her pouch of herbs. If he was hurt, she could help him or take him to a hospital. Mack would go find Sarah if necessary. She saw light from a campfire; the closer she got, the clearer the Confederate uniforms became. She would take the risk and ask them if they knew where the Georgia 53rd was located.

Mack approached cautiously. Sitting near the fire was a man with a long scar on the left side of his face.

"Leonard, I am fine! Stop hovering over me like an old woman," James told him. The corporal had wrapped a bandage around James's left arm. "Are you wounded, corporal?"

"No, sir. Just a small scratch. It would have been my life if you had not grabbed me. I will be forever grateful," Leonard's voice trembled.

"Steady, corporal. We have more fighting ahead of us."

James stood and walked away into the shadows of the night. He couldn't remember how many days he had searched for Mack. He had heard the rumors of the spy that brought information that others had failed to. In his heart he knew this spy, this Night Walker, must be her. The thought of never finding her or the report of her death would be unacceptable. What was it his mother had told them as children? "As long as you have love in your heart, so shall there be hope." James reached into his breast pocket and took out the red paper heart, once more straining to see the faded words written on it. It belongs to you. Mack.

"James, it will always belong to you," Mack told him.

JULY 4

Mack's meeting with James was bittersweet. The news that Sarah was in Gettysburg had not been well received. Mack had planned to stay with James's unit until information arrived about prisoners taken by Union soldiers at a Confederate hospital.

The black of the night was turning into morning when James found Mack with Grey. "Mack, you aren't even sure where Sarah and the others are working. Hospitals have been set up everywhere—barns, houses, churches."

"James, I must go. If they were taken prisoner, I have to help them."

"I could order you to stay," James told her. "You are a Confederate soldier."

"You can order the Night Walker to stay, but Martha Keens is not a soldier at this moment."

James had searched so long it was hard to let her leave. "Go find Sarah, do what you do best, and come back safe. I need you."

Mack knew familiarity would not be proper and circumspect at the moment.

"It's nice to be needed."

She swung into the saddle, and horse and rider disappeared before the sun rose

⤫

Mack changed into Union clothing shortly after leaving James. She then spent the day searching one camp after another for information about Confederate prisoners. She entered the town of Gettysburg, where she was told there might be information at the town newspaper. Mack started to enter the building when the sight of Samuel stopped her. His presence would now force her to alternate locations to obtain information. Night was coming and Mack had been unable to find her friends, which caused frustration and added worry. She could see the fires in the distance. In this camp, Mack found a soldier who had information he was willing to trade for tobacco. After a quick exchange, Mack obtained directions to a place called Monfort Farm. Confederate nurses had been seen there by their scouts.

July 5

Shortly after midnight, Mack left the Union camp and followed the directions she had been given to the Monfort Farm. She did not have to wait long before she saw Sarah and the others tending to the injured that surrounded the farm. Mack was relieved and started to show herself until the next words stopped her.

"Ruby Belle, I am worried about Samuel," Sarah told her.

"Girl, don't you think about that right now. He is probably safe in New York."

"I haven't had a good feeling since he left. What if he is injured? What if he was killed? I will never know."

"You gotta have faith, girl, he'll find you."

Mack turned and headed back to Gettysburg.

⌒

Samuel had finished his report on Gettysburg. The battle had seemed lost at first and then there was a resurgence of the Union. His thoughts now were of Sarah; he must find her. He paced back and forth, over and over, until he finally exploded.

"Dammit, where are you, Sarah?" Samuel's voiced echoed throughout the office.

He turned, and at the back of the office in a dark corner stood a boy in union clothing, who motioned for him to follow. Samuel walked over to the boy.

"I know where Sarah is, Mr. White, and I will take you to her," Mack told him.

Samuel looked down into the face of the Night Walker.

Monfort Farm Confederate Hospital

"Sarah, I need you," Doc Bell called to the woman who had become his right arm.

Sarah and her friends had worked through the night caring for the men that had been stable enough to transfer. She thought about the ones that had been left behind with the promise their injuries would be properly cared for as prisoners of war.

Sarah ran to help as the others made their rounds, inside and outside, where so many men had been brought. Every building on the farm had been used to take care of the wounded.

Maud had been outside checking newly wounded men.

She looked up and couldn't believe the two individuals walking toward the hospital.

"Ruby Belle, come over here. Do you see what is coming up the road?" Maud asked.

"Good Lord."

Both women, along with the twins and Leona, watched as Mack and Samuel came toward them. Leona ran inside to get Sarah.

"Sarah, come, hurry, hurry please!" Leona pulled on Sarah's arm. "You need to come now!"

Sarah had become concerned at the tone of Leona's voice and ran outside to where the others were standing. She then realized what they were looking at. Mack dropped the reins on Grey and started running toward them. Sarah took off running, but an explosion from a smaller building threw everyone to the ground.

"What in God's name was that?" Doc Bell yelled to an orderly. He ran out and saw the bodies of his friends lying everywhere.

"I need some help out here." Doc Bell ran to check on the newly injured at an already overcrowded hospital.

Ruby gathered herself and stood as Doc Bell got to her first.

"Doc, I'm fine. I will go check my girls. I think you better go check on the ones that were closest to the explosion. Damn unexploded shells."

Doc Bell saw Sarah starting to get up. He ran to check on her.

"Sarah, are you hurt?" he asked. "I don't think—"

She saw Mack and Samuel facedown. Sarah screamed their names and pulled away from Doc Bell.

Sarah turned Mack over. There was a bleeding cut across her face. She saw no other injuries.   Mack opened her eyes.

"Grey? Where's Grey?" Mack mumbled.

Maud had made her way to Mack and Sarah. "Sarah, go check on Samuel. I'll take care of Mack. Go, woman, go check on that man." Maud pushed Sarah away.

Doc Bell had turned Samuel over, checking him for injuries, when Sarah made it to his side.

"Sarah, it looks like there are not any immediately life-threatening injuries. I want to get him back to the hospital where we can get a closer look."

"Samuel," Sarah said. She put his head in her lap and leaned over him with tears dropping on his face.

"Lilacs. You smell like lilacs." Samuel opened his eyes and looked at Sarah. "I told you I would come back."

⌇

Doc Bell called for orderlies to come and help carry Samuel back inside where he could closely observe him. He didn't want to alarm Sarah or Samuel, but there might have been injuries he couldn't see, and if that was true, this young man that meant so much to Sarah could be dead in a few days.

⌇

The next days would be the hardest of the war for those who knew and loved Sarah.

Mack had asked Sarah to come and sit with her for a little while.

"Sarah, I have seen James."

"Mack, James is in Georgia," Sarah responded.

"No, he is a lieutenant in the Georgia 53rd."

Sarah was stunned at the news her brother had been so close. She now worried as she knew the war would continue for possibly years.

"Is he well, Mack?" Sarah asked as tears form in the corner of her eyes.

"He's fine."

Mack did not want to tell Sarah about the injuries she had seen on him. "As soon as I am well enough to travel, I am going back and join the 53rd."

"How did you know which hospital I would be working in?" Sarah asked.

"The Night Walker knows everything." Mack paused. "Go check on the reporter. You know he's in love with you."

Sarah left her friend and went to where Samuel had been taken in another part of the hospital. Sarah did not know what she would say to him and was relieved to find him sleeping thanks to Doc Bell. She would check on him later, but now she must go back to the work at hand and those who were more seriously injured.

∽

Samuel seemed to have escaped injury and sat up in his bed, joking and laughing with Sarah the next morning. Leona had brought some food to them. He had just reached for the food when he suddenly coughed and blood began to flow from his mouth.

"Leona, go get Doc Bell," Sarah said.

Doc Bell and Leona returned quickly. He listened to Samuel's chest and looked his body over for injuries that might have finally appeared. He found bruising around the right lower back and in the front above his stomach area.

"What do you think, Doc?" Samuel asked.

"I think you need to rest. Sarah, I need you in the surgery," Doc Bell told her. "Leona will watch Samuel until we come back."

"Don't keep her too long, Doc. We have plans to make," Samuel said as more blood oozed out the left side of his mouth.

Doc Bell took Sarah outside. He had motioned for Ruby, Maud, and the twins to follow them.

"Sarah, yesterday when I first examined Samuel, I was worried that he might have internal injuries. The bleeding and what I found a few moments ago seem to confirm that now," Doc Bell explained gently.

Sarah began to shake, and her knees were giving out. Her friends all stood around her with sympathetic eyes, not knowing what words should be said. She looked up, and Doc Bell kneeled and took her hands.

"Sarah, do you understand? Samuel is probably going to die. You will need to be strong and stay with him. Can you do that?" Doc Bell asked in his most fatherly voice.

"No, you're wrong. He isn't hurt that bad. There are no wounds. You'll see. He'll be fine," Sarah told him, tears running down her face.

"Sarah," Doc Bell began.

"I won't let him die," Sarah screamed and ran toward the stand of trees behind the hospital.

"Dammit, she isn't listening," Doc Bell told the others.

"Doc, there are things that we all must face. Sarah isn't ready to do that," Ruby said.

Sarah ran until she couldn't run anymore, and then sank into the ground. Think, Sarah, think. There is something, there has to be. How can I tell this man that I want to spend the rest of m y life with he is going to die? I can't, I can't.

She took her mother's necklace off and held it in her hands. Please help me. There has to be something I can do, please.

The birds that sat silently in the tree above Sarah were the only ones that shared her sorrow.

⸺

A few minutes later, Sarah looked up to see Leona standing in front of her with the books she had brought from Georgia. "I thought you might need these," Leona said, giving the books to Sarah.

"Who is with Samuel?" Sarah asked.

"Ruby is watching after him. He is sleeping at the moment." Leona walked over and sat down next to Sarah. "Do you re-member the day we came to Waynesboro?" Leona asked.

"Yes," Sarah replied, tears still running down her face.

"Before Ruby and the others found me, many things happened that I never told anyone. This war has touched all of us, Sarah, and for me in a way that I will never forget. I have a story to tell you that I have told no one, not even Ruby.

"Two weeks before I was found, my life was as it had been: happy, a family, a home, no fear. I had been sent to the root cellar with a list for my maw. When I returned, my home was on fire. Yankees stood there laughing at what they had done. They killed my family—mother, father, and my two brothers. I stood and watched, unable to do anything except bury them. The house I was hiding in, dirty and afraid, was my home."

Sarah looked up from her tears at Leona.

"Sarah, you have the opportunity to do something I never could."

"And what is that?"

"You get to say good-bye."

The two sat together for a while. Leona tied Sarah's necklace back around her neck. Sarah couldn't bring herself to give up on Samuel. She read through her books looking for something that would save him.

"Sarah, we need to go back inside. It's getting dark," Leona told her. They both walked back to the hospital, Leona's arm around Sarah's waist.

∽

Sarah went inside to relieve Ruby.

"He's resting," Ruby told Sarah. As she left, Ruby put her hand on Sarah's shoulder.

Sarah sat down, touched her necklace, and called to her mother one more time for strength.

Samuel woke up and looked into Sarah's face.

"Doc Bell came by while you were gone. We had a long talk about my future. I know, Sarah," Samuel told her. "I know."

Sarah moved from the chair to the bed where he was lying.

"Don't leave me, Sarah. I want to spend what time I have left with the woman I have grown to love."

In the darkest of the night with only a candle to light the corner of their world, Sarah placed Samuel's head in her lap. His skin color was becoming pale as more blood came each time he coughed, much of it staining her blue checkered dress. She had nothing to stop the pain he felt. All the knowledge she had could do nothing to help this man who had now become a part of her heart and soul.

"Sarah," Samuel whispered.

Sarah wiped away the blood from his lips. "I'm here," she said.

"Sarah, I have never been a truly religious man, but I know there is something out there for us." Samuel gently placed his hand on Sarah's face. "Promise me, that in the world to come, you will look for me. Promise me."

She looked deep into the face of the man who was dying in her arms. "I promise now and for eternity, I will search for you." She leaned down and kissed him.

Sarah held him to her heart until he took his last breath, just before dawn.

〜

Samuel's death had left everyone within the walls of the hospital solemn. Sarah's friends went about their jobs, caring for the living.

"Maud," a familiar voice called out.

She looked up from changing bandages on an amputee's limb.

"Joseph, is that you?" Maud answered.

"My arm is healing well, thanks to you," Joseph told her. "Where's Samuel? I was told he is here looking for Sarah."

Maud looked at the ground. "I have some bad news."

Sarah had a coffin made to Samuel's height so that his body fit properly and traveled well back to New York. She cleaned and prepared him after death. Leona and the twins searched the fields and streams for tansy and brought it back for Sarah. She rubbed his body with the flowers and placed a wreath she made around his neck to prevent flies from laying eggs on him.

Joseph, Doc Bell, Mack, and the others stood beside Sarah. They watched as she took off the necklace that meant so much to her and placed it in a piece of paper she put inside his shirt pocket. Sarah backed away as the lid was hammered into place and the coffin loaded in the wagon.

Joseph gave Maud an address in New York.

"What's this?" Maud asked.

"Someplace I would like for you to come when this war is over," Joseph told her. "Is that a proposal?"

Joseph never answered, just smiled and started his journey back home with the body of Samuel White.

Doc Bell put his arms around Sarah as they watched the wagon disappear down the road.

"I am truly sorry I could do nothing for that young man."

"I know," Sarah said. "We have work to do."

"Not today. Go and mourn. There will be another day for you to work," Doc Bell told her.

The others walked away, giving their friend the respect and privacy she needed.

Mack walked up and held Sarah's hand. "I have no words to say, my friend," Mack told her.

Sarah turned and hugged Mack tightly. "What are you going to do now?"

"Find James and stay close as I can until the war is over."

"Then go find him and let him know I am alive and doing the work I was born to do."

"If we all live through this hell, I will see you back in Waynesboro."

"Home. Yes, that will be where we will meet, if there is a home to go to after this war," Sarah said softly.

Mack whistled for Grey. She swung her small body into the saddle and then left the Monfort Farm and Sarah.

Chapter 35

New York
White Mansion

The Mansion was quiet and somber. The rooms were filled with mourners and family members. The mirrors had been covered, and yards of black material hung in swags throughout the house, in respect for the dead.

Eric and Franklin slipped away from the continuous stream of mourners and sat in the library together.

"My friend, I do not blame you for the death of my son," Eric began. "This is the life he chose and loved, and he died doing what he wanted."

"He would be alive, here with you, if I had not encouraged him." Franklin was crying.

"No. Samuel would never have stayed here regardless. He was always the rebellious child and went his own way.

"Did you get to see him, Franklin?" Eric asked. "The mortician said that he had been preserved for transport. Do you know who did that? Who was this person that carefully and lovingly prepared my son's body?"

"Yes, I did see him, and I know who sent him back to us. It was a Confederate nurse named Sarah Bowen. Samuel's love for her is why he went back."

Eric poured a drink for himself and Franklin. "Sarah Bowen, you say? Do you have any idea where this young woman is from?" Eric asked.

"I am not sure. Samuel never said. Why?"

"Many years ago, my life was saved by a young man named James Frank Bowen. Out of that one incident, our families became entwined until Eleanor's death."

"Do you think this is the same family?" Franklin asked.

"Samuel was writing to someone for years after his mother died. It could have been the same woman. Julia will know. She is the one who concerns herself with such things."

Julia came to the library in a black mourning gown to find her husband and his friend. "Eric, you and Franklin are being asked for in the main room," Julia told them.

"Julia, do you know the name of the woman Samuel had been receiving letters from?" Eric asked his wife.

"I am not sure of the name, but the letters were from Waynesboro, Georgia."

Both men look at each other, knowing this was the same woman and family connected by bravery and death.

"Julia, I have something that needs to be kept with the family." Franklin reached into his vest pocket and took out the necklace and a piece of paper. He handed it to Julia.

"What is this?" she asked.

"This necklace and note was placed inside Samuel's pocket before he was brought back to New York. Joseph Bines took these from Samuel's pocket for fear they would be stolen. I believe it is something that needs to be kept and passed from generation to generation. It must have a special meaning as I believe it was a gift given heart and soul."

Julia looked at the heart necklace of rose quartz, simple setting, and worn black velvet ribbon; on the back, the letters SJB had been inscribed. The note simply said, I promise. Sarah.

"Eric and Julia, I have an article to write about a man that I want no one to ever forget. I will take my leave of you and your family in your time of grief."

"Franklin, you are family. Never forget that." Eric hugged his old friend.

They left the library, and Julia went upstairs to check on Phillip. She slipped quietly into their bedroom where he slept. She walked over to her Bible and placed the necklace and note in the center. She walked back to her sleeping son, looked down, and softly told him. "You will know of your oldest brother. That is my promise."

Chapter 36

FRANKLIN WEEKLY
NEW YORK
MAY 1865

Franklin Prichard sat at his desk looking at the stories that had been written by other reporters at the Weekly since Samuel's death. He missed that young man every day.

April 9, 1865—Lee surrenders.

April 14, 1865—President Lincoln shot at Ford's Theater.

April 15, 1865—President Lincoln dies, the funeral, swearing in of the new president.

With so much death, it seemed no one was immune.

Franklin opened Samuel's pouch that had been sitting in his office since the day Joseph brought it back with his body. He found Samuel's final notes at Gettysburg. There were a few notes on Sarah Bowen and the nurses who travel. The notes he expected to find on the Night Walker were not there. Franklin assumed Samuel never found the story he wanted, when suddenly he remembered the folder in the safe and quickly turned the combination. He promised to wait until Samuel returned from the war. Now seemed as good a time as any to see what was so very important to Samuel. He took out the folder, sat down with a tall bourbon, and began to read. Samuel had left him the ending, or rather, another chapter about women—the ones who were fighting on the battlefields next to their counterparts. Franklin read these notes until after midnight. The next morning he left the office with a purpose: to fulfill a dream Samuel had had to tell the world about the women that made a difference in the war—the ones who healed and the ones who fought.

Chapter 37

THE ROAD HOME
1865

On the way back to the Bowen farm, after an exhausting war, there was still no rest for the weary. The ladies dropped off Doc Bell in North Carolina at the healing house that was still full of sickness. After ten days filled with healing and sending men home, Maud came around the corner of the house to see Joseph standing with Ruby. Maud had sent a wire to New York telling him where they were headed. She had told him she would come to New York once Sarah was back home. Maud now stood speechless for once in her life.

Sarah stood alone behind the healing house, facing a fire that had been built to burn those things that could cause disease. She held the faded blue-checkered dress that had been stained with so much death. Sarah had rinsed and washed this dress over the years when there was water or a stream. She had held Samuel in this dress, close to her heart, as he died. All that remained was to burn it and keep the small section cut from the bodice.

The week Sarah had planned to stay at the healing house turned into two weeks.

While they were there a letter arrived from Barbara Allen telling Sarah what had happened to Emma. She asked Sarah to pass the information on to Emma's beloved, Leonard.

Edith, Doc Bell, Joseph, and Maud walked out to the wagon with Sarah.

"Y'all take care, you hear?" Maud told Sarah, hugging each of her friends.

"Are you two going back to New York?" Leona asked.

"No, I told Franklin that I would not be coming back," Joseph told them.

"We are going to stay here and start a life together," Maud said. "I am young enough to make a good wife and, Lord willing, a mother."

Joseph's face turned red as they all laughed.

∽

When they finally arrived back in Georgia, Sarah and her friends entered what looked like a new gate on her parents' farm. She began to breathe rapidly as she couldn't see the home she'd left, but something much bigger.

"Ruby, my home. What happened here while we were all gone?" Sarah asked a question no one in the wagon could answer.

"Steady, woman. We will get the answers you need."

The noise of horses and a wagon had caused another to take notice and come to the door of the barn.

Sarah and the others got out of the wagon. She walked up and looked at this big house and could only think of all that had been lost.

The figure in the barn walked up, unheard, behind Sarah and the others.

"Hello, sis. It's almost finished."

Sarah turned. "Ethan."

After Sarah hugged and kissed her brother, she began to ask questions.

"What happened to the house, Ethan? Do you know? How long have you been here? Have you seen James?" Sarah asked so many questions so quickly Ethan backed away.

"Sis, I think it would be better if Uncle Mike and Aunt Lilly fill in the holes here. We have only been home a month."

"We?" Sarah asked, hoping James and Mack were here.

"My wife, Deanna, and our son, Raymond Alexander. He was born the day the South surrendered. I wanted to come home, so we left the first of June. Sis, can we do this later?" Ethan asked.

Sarah turned around to see her friends standing there. "Ethan, these are my friends, nurses who I worked and traveled with during the war," Sarah said.

Introductions were made, and Ethan helped everyone back into the wagon. He took the reins, and they made another trip to see more family down the road. Sarah looked at the man that sat next to her and saw something familiar: his smile—the same as their mother's.

Aunt Lilly and Uncle Mike came running out of the house when they arrived. Tears of joy and happiness were the first order of the moment. Sarah made introductions again so that no one would be left out of the homecoming.

"Sarah, where's Mack?" Aunt Lilly asked.

"I was hoping she and James were already here."

"She?" Aunt Lilly asked.

Sarah smiled; happy she did not have to pretend any longer. "Yes, Mack is a woman."

"Lord, do tell!" Aunt Lilly went on.

Ethan had disappeared into the house and returned with his wife and child. Deanna walked out to where Sarah stood, and hugged and kissed her. She handed Raymond to Sarah.

"Meet your Aunt Sarah, Ray," Deanna told her small son.

Sarah took her nephew, kissed him, and looked at the lovely young woman who had become a part of the Bowens' family. Deanna was tall like Ethan, with freckles across her nose and a smile that brightened the day.

"Come inside, all of you. We'll need to find beds and start some dinner. Sarah, there is so much to tell you, and I have so many questions," Aunt Lilly began.

"Girl, it's good to have you home." Uncle Mike hugged her.

Sarah tried to take in the questions and looked at the crowd of people coming into the house.

"It's good to be home, isn't it?" Leona asked.

"Yes, it is, and I hope you will call this home, too," Sarah told her.

⟳

Over the next month, neighbors and family worked on the big house to get it finished before winter. The story of Sherman and his men burning down the house and crops sent chills down Sarah's back. The slaves once owned were now free. Uncle Mike offered those still on the farm a place to stay and a fair wage for their work. Uncle Mike's house was spared and all the bedrooms were filled with family and visitors until homes were finished. It was now the first of December; furniture had been made, curtains hung, and cupboards filled with supplies. There was a larger warming cupboard made just for Sarah. The time had come for Ruby and her daughters to leave.

"Ruby, I wish you would stay until the spring. The weather could be bad along the way to New Orleans," Sarah told her.

"Woman, we still got friends between here and there. We'll be fine."

Sarah knew Ruby and her daughters could take care of themselves. "I want you to write to me, keep in touch. We have been through too much."

Ruby laughed. "I think we can do that. Sarah, thank you for leaving your home, teaching, healing, and caring. You have sacrificed much for all of us."

Sarah hugged Ruby and the twins. "I will be waiting for those letters."

"Leona, you take care of Sarah," Sadie told her.

"I will."

"Sarah, we're going to miss you," Sallie said. Sarah waved as the women from New Orleans left the Bowen farm. She stood and watched until they disappeared.

"Leona, time to go into our home," Sarah said.

Leona smiled, and they went into the big house.

Chapter 38

THE BIG HOUSE
CHRISTMAS 1865

Sarah once again worked in the root cellar attempting to straighten, clean, and prepare for the spring.

Leona and Deanna saw strangers approaching the house. Three weary travelers entered through the gate. It was early Christmas morning.

"Deanna, go and find Ethan. I will find Sarah," Leona told her.

Deanna took the baby and went to the barn where Ethan had been working. Leona ran out the back door to the cellar.

"Sarah, come now. There are people coming, and I don't recognize them."

"It will be fine."

Sarah took the gun from her pocket and left the cellar. Both women walked around the front of the house. Ethan had sent Deanna and the baby to hide. He had taken a pitchfork and run to the front of the house to join the two women.

"Thank you, God in heaven, thank you," Sarah said. She knew James's horse Grey, and the only person that could ride him, besides James, was Mack. Sarah gave Leona the gun and began to run. "James, Mack, welcome home, welcome home!"

"I don't believe you will need that, brother," James told him.

Ethan dropped the only thing he had for a weapon and hugged his brother.

"I will be back in a minute." Ethan left and ran back to the barn.

James turned to Sarah. "What the hell is this?" He pointed to the house that stood before him.

"It's home. I'll explain later," Sarah said. She saw the long scar across the left side of his face and knew the war had left its mark on them all. Sarah then hugged Mack, picking her up off the ground.

"Where did Ethan go?" James asked.

"To get my family," Ethan said.

James turned to see a woman and child walking toward him. "You've grown up, I see."

"Yes, I have."

"Leonard, will you take the horses to the barn and make sure they are watered, fed, and brushed?" James ordered.

"Yes sir, Captain." Leonard quickly took the animals away.

"Captain?" Ethan asked.

"A story for another time, not now," James told him. "I want to go inside, clean up, eat, and sleep in a bed."

"Merry Christmas, everyone," Leona said.

⌒

It had taken just a few days for everyone to settle into the house and find their own place.

Mack shared a room with Leona for the moment, until she and James were properly married. Sarah had heard Leona attempt to talk Mack into wearing a dress shortly after they arrived. The argument was short, and Mack exited their room in pants, shirt, and braces. Mack's next request was a short haircut. Other than that, Sarah was pleased to see that the two got along; she had heard them talking late at night when they should have been asleep.

Sarah had come to the kitchen to start breakfast and found old habits did not change. James was up at first light and had made coffee. He poured his sister a cup, and they sat at the breakfast table. "James, who is that young man with you? Leonard, I believe you called him."

"Leonard Williams—good man, good friend. We went through a lot during the war. I am hoping he will stay and help work the farm. Why are you asking?"

"I believe I have a letter from a young woman who was his love. She died, drowned after she gave birth to a still born," Sarah said.

"My God, Sarah, I cannot imagine all you have been through and seen. I am sorry for all that happened between us the day I left."

Sarah reached for her brother and kissed him. "Time gone. All that matters now are those here, the family. I must tell Leonard about Emma."

"Leonard never mentioned her to me. Do you want me to be with you when you tell him?" James asked.

"I think that might make him more comfortable."

James got another cup of coffee. "I'll go get him." James went out to the barn where he had sent Leonard earlier to help Ethan.

Leonard knocked on the door when he arrived at the house. "Miss Sarah, it's Leonard. The Captain sent me to talk to you about Emma."

"Come in, Leonard. Coffee?" Sarah asked. "Yes, thank you kindly."

Sarah got him coffee and the letter she had carried with her through the war and back.

James returned to the kitchen as Sarah started to talk.

"Sarah, I think you better sit down," James told his sister. "Go ahead, Leonard. Tell Sarah what you told me in the barn."

"Miss Sarah, I had a brother named Leon who was a year older. He was married to a woman named Emma. Leon was killed on his farm just before I left to go fight the Yankees. Leon and I looked alike, and Emma was always kidding us. I didn't know she was gonna have a baby. She lost her mind when Leon died, kept asking me why I was leaving her, didn't I love her anymore, crazy things. When I left Alabama, she was staying with her sister. That's the last I heard of her until today," Leonard finished.

Sarah remembered how Emma cared for the wounded at the healing house. How could she have not seen this woman's pain? She handed Leonard the letter. He read the note and looked at James, then Sarah.

"Captain, please believe me. Emma was not betrothed to me, and that baby was my brother's," Leonard said again as tears fell.

"I believe you," Sarah said and gave him the letter from Barbara Allen.

"I just can't believe she didn't tell anyone about the baby. Her family would have seen to them," Leonard said.

The mind will take a tragedy and hide it away until it can face the truth. Sarah remembered the words of Barbara Allen the day they left Emma in her care.

"It's all right, Leonard. You can go on out and help Ethan," James told him.

"Thank you, Captain and you, too, Miss Sarah," Leonard responded; then he quickly left the house.

"Emma had been so sincere about her love for Leonard and the baby. How did I miss this?" she asked her brother.

"Sarah, with all that happens to folks, you can't see everything. You've done all you can, but this time you have to let it go."

Mack came to the kitchen in her homespun britches and shirt, barefoot, hair matted to one side from sleep. Sarah noticed the smile on James's face.

"What's all the noise?" Mack asked.

Sarah looked at her brother. "I think it's time the family had a meeting."

Chapter 39

Life Renewed
January 1866

*A new year and the family had gathered in the big house for fel-*lowship and announcements. The Bowen families had grown, and plans were discussed on how to proceed now that the war had ended. The Bowen legacy would survive with hard work, and the farms would once again prosper. There would be time in the future to talk and share what had passed.

"I would like for everyone to come to the main room," James called.

Two fireplaces warmed the main room and all who sat. Hands were joined and heads bowed for silent prayers.

"Today we give thanks for all who have returned home safely, for the land which has been burned but not destroyed, and for the generations to come. Amen."

"Amen."

"I now want to ask Mack Keens if she will be my wife, and if she'll marry me on Valentine's Day." James smiled.

"I didn't think you were ever going to ask me. I will marry you as long as I can still wear pants," Mack told him.

The room broke out in laughter.

"I think I can deal with a wife in pants," James said.

The rest of the day the women talked of the wedding and plans that must be made quickly.

The men had gone outside to sample the newest brew from Uncle Mike.

"James, I need to find a place to build a home for my family," Ethan told his brother.

"I know, and there is a section of land that I was saving for you," James responded.

"Uncle Mike, how soon could I get some help from you to begin building?" Ethan asked.

Uncle Mike finished his drink from the jug. "If the weather holds, we can start clearing the land next week."

Ethan smiled.

"That wife of yours wants her own place, does she?" Uncle Mike chuckled.

"It's time," Ethan told him.

"Agreed, we all need our own home. I will make the arrangements," Uncle Mike told Ethan.

"Deanna's father is a merchant and her dowry was substantial, even in war." Ethan walked away and went into the house to give the news to his wife.

James, have you got a minute?" Uncle Mike asked. "Is that young man, Leonard, still sleeping in your barn?"

"I can't get him to come inside."

"Lil and I have been talking, and we have room. We'd like to have him stay with us. Of course, he will have to work and help out," Uncle Mike told his nephew.

"You will never have to tell him to work. He's a good man and honest."

"Good to know. Figured as much or you never would have let him come home with you," Uncle Mike told James. "You really going to marry that spitfire of a girl?"

"Yes, I'm really going to marry her."

"Think I liked her better when I thought she was a boy." Uncle Mike slurred the last few words.

James just laughed and headed to the house to find Leonard to tell him the good news.

Valentine's Day
Methodist Church
Waynesboro

Sarah, Leona, and Mack stood in a room at the pastor's house. Mack looked out the window at the people that continued to arrive at the church. Deanna took care of all the arrangements; she found flowers and decorated the church and helped with the food to feed the crowd that continued to grow. Mack paced the house.

"Sarah, I ain't gonna be able to get on with this. I... I...can'ts do it," Mack fumbled.

"What has happened to the woman that I knew a week ago? Calm down. These are your friends, our family. The three of us will be standing right next to you," Sarah told her.

The knock on the door meant the time had come. Sarah opened the door. Doc Bell walked into the house. "Time to go, ladies."

They all walked to the church and waited for the doors to open. Each of them wore their Sunday best dress. As the doors opened, the music being played changed to the song that Mack had requested, "The Soldier's Wife." Deanna and Leona took their places at the front of the church. Sarah stood looking at the full pews of family and friends. She walked toward the front looking at James, Ethan, Leonard, and Joseph all in new suits. Sarah saw Mack and Doc Bell take their place.

⌒

James looked at the tiny figure at the back of the church, the woman with her short hair, in a white dress that showed the figure she tried so hard to hide. James smiled as she walked down the aisle with Doc Bell, knowing that tomorrow Mack would be wearing pants.

The preacher took his cue. "Who gives this woman in marriage?"

Doc Bell answered, "I do, for her family."

He walked up to James, gave him Mack's hand, patted him on the back, and said, "Good luck, son."

The entire church filled with laughter, and Sarah saw Mack's shoulders relax.

∽

The afternoon turned into evening as bride and groom were sent off to a private place in Waynesboro for the night. Sarah, Maud, and Edith attempted to put away food and clean the big house.

"Sarah, I cannot believe all the folks that were at the church and here today," Maud said.

"What did James do in the war?" Joseph asked.

"I honestly do not know. I have never asked. It seems to be a very personal thing with him for now," Sarah told them.

"The scar on his face told a story of its own," Doc Bell told the group.

Sarah's friends from the healing house began to discuss their return home tomorrow. She did not want to think about them leaving and walked into the main room where Leonard had been sitting with Leona. Deanna and Ethan chaperoned and smiled as she came to the door. Leonard saw Sarah and stood.

"Miss Sarah, may I have a moment of your time?" Leonard asked.

Sarah smiled. "Yes."

Sarah took her shawl and walked out on the porch. The evening was cold, but Sarah would give this young man his time to talk.

"Miss Sarah, I would like to have your permission to call on Miss Leona," Leonard began. "I will be a man of honor."

"Leonard, I believe you, and yes, you may call on Leona," Sarah told him.

Leonard's grin became so wide it covered his face. "Thank you," he told her, then almost tore the door off in his excitement as he went back inside to tell Leona.

Sarah looked at the sky with stars so bright she could touch them.

"Come on, Leonard. It's time to go," Uncle Mike said loudly.

"Michael, you are too rough with that boy," Aunt Lilly chastised him.

"Yes, sir. I am right behind you and Ms. Lilly," Leonard answered.

"Sarah, I guess we will have another job watching those two until a wedding is called for," Uncle Mike laughed as he helped his wife into the wagon.

Leona had walked out to wave good-bye to Leonard. Sarah watched the small exchange and thought of how the smallest gestures mean so much.

May
Big House

Sarah walked out on the large porch of the big house to a beautiful morning. Winter had turned to spring and now summer was only a few weeks away. She watched James as he waited for his wife to swing into the saddle so they could check the fields. The two had settled into married life quite easily since the wedding.

"Sarah, don't hold dinner for us. We won't be back until dark," James said.

"Sis, I need to talk to you later," Mack told Sarah. "Nothing special, just woman talk."

"I will be here or in the cellar. Leona and I have work to do," Sarah replied.

Mack swung into her saddle. James smiled as they rode out the gate to the flourishing fields of tobacco.

Ethan and Deanna's house would be finished in a few days. Sarah would be sad to see them leave, especially Ray, but understood that everyone needed their own home.

Sarah stood thinking of how so many things had transpired since the end of the war. There were still scars upon the land and its people, but in time they would mend. She walked out to her garden and smiled at the wonder of nature and its power to heal.

CHRISTMAS

Sarah could hardly believe it had been only a year since the family was reunited. They gathered again to share what they had with family and friends.

"James, can I talk to you for a moment?" Uncle Mike asked.

The two walked out the back door to talk.

"This must be important," James responded.

"That young man Leonard came to me about a month ago and purchased ten acres of land three miles from my house. I believe there is about to be another wedding," Mike told him.

"Well, then I guess we better help him. Leonard should be warned that womenfolk can be a bit hard to get along with sometimes." James laughed and the two went back inside.

Mack had found Sarah in the kitchen with Deanna. "Sarah, I need to talk to you for a minute."

Sarah turned around to see the color drain from Mack's face. Leona came in just as Mack began to fall to the floor. The three women caught her and all sat on the floor. Sarah cradled Mack in her arms.

"I'll get James," Deanna told Sarah.

Sarah reached out and stopped Deanna from leaving. "Wait, I think I may know why she fainted. She may not be ready to tell James just yet," Sarah told her.

"You think she is going to have a baby, don't you, Sarah?" Leona asked.

"What the hell just happened to me, Sarah?" Mack looked up at her friends.

"How long have you not felt well?" Sarah asked.

"I have been sick for almost two months. Am I going to die?"

Sarah, Deanna, and Leona all laughed. "No, you are not going to die. You are going to make James a father."

Chapter 40

FULL CIRCLE
1867

The people of Waynesboro began to call upon Sarah once again as their healer. Sarah and Leona worked together to care for those in their community. Leona learned quickly, and her healing abilities improved daily. This day started early for Sarah, as she had just finished delivering a neighbor's second baby when word was sent about a child with a broken arm. Sarah smiled and took the two chickens and a small sack of flour as her payment. She then traveled to where she set the broken arm, placed comfrey on it, and then left herbs for the fever the child would have from the injury. The family gave her sugar and coffee. She appreciated the way people paid for her services, though she had never requested it. The day had been long, and she would be glad to see her home and family. Sarah rode up to the house and saw Leonard and Leona sitting with Mack. The two helped her out of the chair.

"Sis, I am glad to see you," Mack told her. "I'm tired but didn't want to leave these two alone. I will leave them with you." Mack waddled off in a day wrapper since her pants no longer fit. She would go for a nap before dinner.

Sarah smiled when she heard Mack cursing about her size and being hot as she walked away.

"Miss Sarah." Leonard tipped his hat. "I would like to talk to you before James gets in from the fields." He came to the wagon and helped Sarah out.

"Leonard, can you bring the supplies inside and take the chickens around back to the pens, please? Is this something James and I should be hearing together?" Sarah asked.

"I'm not sure, but I want to ask you first." Leonard's face turned red.

"Ask her," Leona said as she elbowed him.

"I would like yours and the Cap.. James's permission to marry Leona." Leonard's voice quivered.

Sarah had known this was coming. She just thought it would be before now.

"Why don't you stay for dinner and ask me again when James comes in from the fields?" Sarah said.

Leonard wiped the sweat off his brow.

"Yes, ma'am, I will do that."

∽

The evenings were nice just before summer came to stay. James arrived home just as dinner was being set on the table. He went to clean the dust away and woke his pregnant wife. They both returned to an added guest. Leonard stood as Mack came to the table.

"Good evening, Leonard. It's nice to see you. Sit down," James said.

The meal progressed with little conversation. Leonard had sweat running down his face even though the evening air felt cool coming through the open windows and door.

"James, I believe Leonard has something he would like to ask us," Sarah said.

"Is this true?" James asked.

"Yes, sir," Leonard answered.

"Then let's get to it, shall we? Sarah, you can leave the table to Mack and Leona." James stood and went to the main room.

James and Sarah sat down, but Leonard started to pace in front of them. He seemed shaky.

"Leonard, do you have something to say or are you just going to wear the floor out?"James asked.

"Miss Sarah, James, I would like your permission to marry Leona," Leonard began.

James knew what this young man had done to prepare for this day, and he would allow him time to impress both of them.

"I bought land last October from Mr. Mike. I paid him cash, so I own it outright. I have cleared the land, built a home, and have a job. I have no debt and have saved a little bit. I have done this so that I would not come empty-handed to ask for Leona's hand in marriage."

James saw Leona standing around the corner listening to Leonard.

"The thing I haven't heard is whether or not you love her," James told him.

"I care about Leona the same way you love Mack. I can't imagine living without her in my life another day. We want children, and to continue to work the land and be part of this family that has given us so much."

"I guess there is just one thing left to do," James told him.

"And when will this marriage take place?" Sarah asked.

"Christmas, here in the big house," Leona yelled from around the corner. "If that's all right with you."

"I guess that settles the question. Then my answer is yes," Sarah said.

"How can I go against my own sister?" James said.

"Sarah, I have a problem," Mack called from the kitchen.

Sarah got up and went to check on her.

"I'm all wet," Mack told her.

James came to the kitchen and saw his wife standing in a puddle of fluid.

"What—?" James started to ask.

Sarah hoped that Mack was wrong on her missed cycles or this baby would be too early.

"Mack, your water has broken. James, this could be a long night for all of us," Sarah told him. "Leonard, when you go home tonight, please tell Aunt Lilly I will need her in the morning after Uncle Mike leaves for the field. Then go to Ethan's and tell Deanna to come and bring Ray with her.

"Yes, ma'am," Leonard answered and left the house.

Sarah remembered what happened to Emma and could see the concern in Leona's eyes.

"Leona, this is not the same as Emma. We have taken good care of Mack. She eats well and rests when we tell her. I thought this might happen since she is a small woman. Mack's cycles were not regular since the war. She could be wrong about them and when she became with child. This baby could be ready to be born. We will all do what we can to make sure this baby makes it to this world safe," Sarah reassured her.

James now paced the floor outside his and Mack's room. Sarah walked out and ran into him.

"James, she isn't dying, and the pains haven't started yet. She would do better with you in there anyway. Mack is the same person she was a few hours ago," Sarah said sternly.

"What do I say to her?" James asked.

"The same things you two say to each other every night."

James went into the bedroom with his wife.

"James, can you give me some of those rags there? Sarah said the water would just keep coming, and it seems to be a lot." Mack looked up at him.

"Well, Sarah was right. Nothing is different yet." James smiled and got the rags she had asked for.

◊

Two days later, just before dawn, Amanda Elise was born, healthy and, as Sarah had thought, due.

Mack's birthing went well and quickly once the pains began. James surprised everyone and never left his wife's side. He decided if he could handle the horrors of war, he could handle the birth of his child. Deanna and Leona cleaned and straightened the room while Sarah helped Mack place Amanda to nurse. Mother, father, and baby were left alone. As Sarah closed the door, she watched Mack lay in the curve of James's strong arm, holding his family close to his heart. Aunt Lilly had made coffee and breakfast for those in the house. Sarah took her cup and walked out into the beauty of the morning. She stood alone as tears finally flowed—the ones she had held back for such a long time. This was the first time Sarah had cried for Samuel.

BIG HOUSE
CHRISTMAS CELEBRATION

Franklin Prichard was standing at the door of a huge home, where he had been told Sarah Bowen and her family lived. He knew it was Christmas, but this was the only time he could get away from the office. Franklin had finished the task he began over a year ago. Samuel's book had been finished and requests for a second printing were on his desk to be sent to the publisher. The money had been placed in trust as directed by Samuel before he left New York for Gettysburg. He was not sure how to approach Sarah or what he would say when he did find her. Franklin felt that Sarah needed to know just how special she was to Samuel. There were papers that must be signed and returned to New York. Franklin would not take too much of her time. He knocked on the door.

"Hello, can I help you?" Sarah looked at him as a stranger but appeared to know him the moment he began to speak.

"I am looking for Sarah Jane Bowen. I am—"

"Franklin Prichard of the Franklin Weekly from New York," Sarah answered, stepping aside and smiling. "Will you please come inside?"

Franklin entered and became aware that something special was taking place in this house. There were children, babies, a bride and groom, people everywhere celebrating, music playing, and a table of food that made his mouth water. He had intruded.

"I am sorry I have come at a bad time," Franklin apologized.

"Nonsense, how can you say that? Please come and join us. There is so much I wish to ask you about Samuel. James, Ethan, we have company," Sarah called to her brothers and family. Franklin was welcomed into the Bowen home and treated like an old friend.

He now saw why Samuel fell in love with this woman. Sarah was lovely; she wore a dress that matched her blue eyes. He couldn't understand how they could still sparkle after seeing the pain and the horrors of the war. Her hair shined like the sun, and she smelled of lilacs. The day Franklin had feared and dreaded had become a wonderful surprise. His heart felt light for the first time since Samuel's funeral. The music continued, and he ate until there was no more room in his stomach and truly laughed. The newlyweds were sent off in fashion for the night; children and babies were put to bed, dishes cleaned, and family on their way home or to the barn to sleep wrapped in quilts made with love. Franklin joined the men outside for some of Uncle Mike's best. He was sure he would never be ill again as anything bad in his body was destroyed after the last pass of the jug.

As the men came back inside, Franklin walked over to Sarah. "I would like to talk to you and your family. It is of some importance."

"First, I have already prepared a room for you to stay the night, and I will not take no for an answer."

"After the last drink of Uncle Mike's brew, I gladly accept your hospitality."

James had added wood to the fireplaces in the main room. Mack, Ethan, Deanna, and Sarah had all come and found a place to sit. They listened to what this man from New York had to say to their family.

"I want to thank all of you for a wonderful day. It had been too long since I have found the joy of laughter among friends. I have several things to say and a few questions. Samuel was working on a story about the Night Walker before he died. I cannot find any notes. Sarah, do you know where he might have left them? Maybe with you?" Franklin asked.

"No, I don't have them," she replied. "Do you have any information about this spy?" Franklin asked.

"I believe I can answer your questions about the Night Walker," James told him.

Everyone in the room looked at James.

"The day the south surrendered, a young man was brought into our camp seriously injured. You remember me telling you about him, Martha."

"Yes, about fourteen years old, from Alabama, is that correct?" Mack answered.

"I had seen my share of death, mind you, but for this young boy to die that day was so sad and such a waste of life. We had no medical help available. He refused to tell me his name, just where he was from. Going through his belongings, I found information that led me to believe he had been the spy called the Night Walker. There were handwritten notes, maps, a Union uniform. I burned everything."

"Pity. That story would have topped the Gray Ghost," Franklin told him. "But the main reason for my visit to Waynesboro was to find you, Sarah. Samuel was a wonderful writer, reporter, and the closest thing to a son I will ever have in my life. He became so involved in the war and the horror of it he took a personal interest in the women that gave a part of their lives to help. The women that traveled to the battlefields and placed themselves in danger to save lives were his main interest. Sarah, were you aware of the special series he was writing about?"

"Yes, he interviewed all of us that were there helping for his story," Sarah answered.

"After his death, I discovered another section of his papers about the women soldiers. It took me over a year to finish his work—interviewing, proving what he had written and personally observed. In October of 1866, his stories were published in book form." Franklin took a book out of his case and handed it to Sarah.

The Women Who Travel in War, written by Eric Samuel White Jr. and Franklin Alfred Prichard.

Sarah opened the book. It was dedicated to the memory of Eric Samuel White Jr., who paid the ultimate price. Tears gathered in the corners of her eyes.

"Sarah, look at the next page," Franklin instructed.

To Sarah:

The woman that opened m y eyes and stole m y heart.

Forever yours,

Samuel

Tears ran down her face. Deanna handed Sarah a handkerchief. Mack put her arm around Sarah's shoulder.

"I am aware that you and Samuel knew each other long before you met. Once he met you, watched you work and heal, he fell in love with you. He felt what you had to offer to the world was important. Samuel knew the art of healing was worth teaching to others who wished to learn. Samuel was wealthy, and his family is wealthy. The money from his stories and this book was placed in a trust. Half of the money is for the education of nurses in the north. The other half is for you, Sarah, so that you can teach the art of healing through nature. He also left you half of his inheritance."

James cleared his throat. "Mr. Prichard."

"Franklin. James, please call me Franklin."

"Franklin, how much money are we talking about?"

"With what I have in trust at this time and sales of the book already in its second printing, over fifty thousand dollars at this point. The amount will continue to increase as time goes by."

"And the half of his inheritance?" Ethan asked.

"Two hundred and fifty thousand," Franklin answered.

Sarah stood and started to leave the main room, then fainted.

∾

Franklin Prichard stayed with the Bowens until the beginning of the New Year, 1868. He and Sarah spent hours talking about Samuel and his family and about their time together in the war. He never told her he took her necklace and gave it to his family.

"Franklin, I will never be able to thank you for this gift," Sarah told him.

"It is you I want to thank. I now have two families, Samuel's and yours. I hope you will allow me to come back again."

"You will always be welcome in the Bowen home."

"Then I will take my leave in the morning and go back to New York. There are papers to file with the solicitors, and you have a school to build," Franklin said.

∾

The next morning, James, Mack, and Amanda were waiting in the wagon for Franklin. They would take him to Augusta and then pick up supplies.

"James, you know Sarah actually did burn Samuel's notes to protect me," Mack told him.

"The Night Walker is dead, never to be resurrected," James said as he kissed his wife.

∾

Sarah hugged Franklin at the front door. "Thank you for everything," she said.

"No, thank you for loving and healing," Franklin told her. "I will see you again. I promise."

Franklin was good on his word and returned when Sarah opened her school, in the summer of 1868. Ruby Belle and the twins moved to Waynesboro at Sarah's request.

The school quickly outgrew the need for only one instructor, and Sarah could not give equally to her job as healer and teacher. Ruby was more than happy to come back to see her friend and help. For the rest of her life, Sarah taught and continued to be the healer in Waynesboro.

∽

When Sarah died before her time, many said it was from working too hard in the community. There were others that said she died due to the harshness of the war.

She was buried next to her parents in the family cemetery on the farm. Sarah's family, which included many nephews and nieces, stood at her gravesite to say good-bye.

James and Mack stayed a moment longer after the others had left. Mack was not ready to leave the woman who had changed her life. James knew his wife all too well and went to the wagon to wait. When she had said her farewell, Mack walked to meet her husband. James helped her up, and as they left, he asked a question that had been troubling him through the many years since the war.

"Mack, do you know what happened to Sarah's heart?"

"She gave it away...at Gettysburg."

Epilogue

 ❦

There have been many stories about ghosts that walk the battle-
fields at Gettysburg. If you should find yourself there at dusk
on sacred ground, take time to listen. There could be the sound
of artillery or the smell of gunpowder in the air around you.
The chill in the heat of a summer night might be due to the
screams of injured and dying men. Remember, you are in good
company with those who came before us. The sounds of horses
and men in full charge are powerful reminders of all that took
place during those three days.

There are specters that still guard picket lines, and men
laughing around campfires that can be seen only from the corner
of your eye. Closer to the hospitals, men come to look for what
was taken from them and discarded. Many of these spirits do
not realize they are no longer a part of the present, and still they
linger. They stay to remind us of the terrible price that was paid
on both sides.

The spirit of Sarah Bowen has been seen walking the same
battlefields, at the hospitals where she worked to save the
dying. She searches for what was taken away—the love that
was denied.

She still hears the call of wars and follows it away from this place to strange lands to look for that which was lost and given away. You will know her, for she still wears the blue-checkered dress with pink flowers, stained with the blood of those she tried to save—the blood of Samuel.

Sarah keeps the promise she made to search for eternity, for there will be no peace until she finds her heart and the man who was meant to have it.

Coming Soon in the Look for Me Series

SUNDAY, NOVEMBER 30, 1941
HONOLULU, HAWAII

"Lawrence, may I speak with you for a moment?" Jefferson asked his son over breakfast.

"Go ahead," Larry responded. He was thankful his mother and sister left early to go to the beach. He had always hated these types of conversations with his father.

"I have been invited next Sunday to a breakfast at the naval base. Your mother has indicated that she abhors these kinds of things and wishes to stay here. Would you be interested in joining me?" Jefferson asked.

Larry was thrilled to get an opportunity to be part of what might be a story, but played it easy so his father would not be suspicious."I would be honored, Father."

Jefferson looked up at his son. "It will be a suit-and-tie meeting. I assume you still own one, though I have not seen you properly dressed since we arrived," Jefferson said.

"Yes, Father, I still own a suit and tie. I'm surprised that you have not enjoyed the casual dress of the island. I have no intentions of embarrassing you or your name," Larry answered.

"I would say it is our family name, but since you have chosen not to use it, I do not feel the need to worry on how it reflects upon me, except this time," Jefferson told him.

"Fine, Father, what time and where?" Larry had had enough. He didn't understand why all their conversations ended this way.

"Next Sunday, the seventh. We need to leave by 5:30 a.m. sharp," Jefferson said.

"I will be ready, in suit and tie. Do you have a shirt color picked out for me, too?" Larry asked.

This ended the breakfast conversation between father and son.

DECEMBER 7, 1941 5:00 A.M.

Larry adjusted his red necktie and made sure there would be no complaint or criticism by his father this morning. He picked up his jacket and slipped it over his tall frame. He reached to put his cigarettes in the same pocket as the heart necklace, and then changed his mind. He placed them in his shirt pocket instead. There was a knock on his door.

I knew it. Father is always early. "Just a moment, Father, I need to get my keys," Larry told him as he opened the door.

Jefferson was surprised and pleased his son had become the responsible adult he expected.

"You made a good choice this morning, Lawrence. I would have chosen a darker necktie," Jefferson said.

"This is the only necktie I brought with me," Larry answered.

Once downstairs, both men were ushered into a military car that waited for them. The drive to the base would be a short one.

They were checked through the gate of the Ford Island Naval Air Station and continued to their intended destination.

Once they were inside the private military housing, it became apparent this was what Larry had expected, a private breakfast meeting. He knew his mother was all too familiar with these types of dealings. There were some contracts made in private before they were brought to the forefront of the government. Larry's father had what the military needed— steel—and there was a price to pay for those needs. He knew the only story here would be what had been served for breakfast. Any report of conversation could result in men dressed in dark suits visiting his boss at the newspaper.

Breakfast began promptly at 0630 military time.

"Jefferson, how is Jean?" the general asked.

"She is well, thank you for asking. She and my daughter had beach plans today or they would be here this morning," Jefferson told him.

"The weather report I received indicates a beautiful day for their excursion," the general responded.

This went on for about an hour. Larry needed a cigarette before he was subjected to more uninteresting conversation.

"Gentlemen, if you will excuse me for a moment, I need to step outside," Larry said.

Jefferson nodded his head. The other men acknowledged Larry as he left the table.

Larry exited out the side doors. As he walked toward the water on another beautiful morning, Larry longed to be surfing. He was thankful for the opportunity that brought him to Hawaii. Larry looked at the ships on "Battleship Row" and could see the men of the USS Arizona beginning morning duties. It was 0755 when Larry struck a match to light his cigarette, but before he could get the fire to his smoke, the first bomb exploded. The match burned down and blistered his finger before he realized what had just happened. The screams of men began; voices gave orders, sirens howled from ships and the base, and gunfire erupted, along with fire, which caused thick black smoke to rise, erasing the sun from the sky. Larry tried to take in the horror that appeared before him. The planes that attacked the ships had familiar markings, markings he knew well from reports and photos at the paper. Japan had attacked Pearl Harbor. He started to turn around when the next bomb struck too close and knocked him to his back; light turned to dark.

The black smoke rolled across the base like night. Larry opened his eyes and could not believe what was before him. His head lay in the lap of a beautiful woman. She looked down with the bluest eyes; her hair was the color of the sun, and her dress blue checkered with small pink flowers. He could see the dress was stained with blood, but the scent of lilacs engulfed them. She leaned down, kissed him tenderly, and then placed her hands on his face. Her voice was soothing but with such need when she whispered in his ear.

"Wait for me. Promise that you will wait for me."

Those were the last words he heard as she faded away, along with his sight.

It matters not who the person is, its what you can do to ease their suffering.

Empty the Heart of All the Bad —
Heal the heart and mend the Soul